Books by Shirley Rousseau Murphy

The Grass Tower
Silver Woven in My Hair
The Pig Who Could Conjure the Wind
The Flight of the *Fox*
Soonie and the Dragon
The Ring of Fire
The Wolf Bell
The Castle of Hape

THE Castle of Hape

by

Shirley Rousseau Murphy

Atheneum * *New York*

1980

LIBRARY OF CONGRESS CATALOGING IN PUBLICATION DATA

Murphy, Shirley Rousseau.
The castle of Hape.

(An Argo book)
Sequel to The Wolf Bell
SUMMARY: The great dark power of the monster Hape blinds
the farseeing minds of the Seers of Carriol
so they can only grope against the growing evils around them.
[1. Fantasy] I. Title.
PZ7.M956Cas [Fic] 79-22764
ISBN 0-689-30753-5

Published simultaneously in Canada by
McClelland & Stewart, Ltd.
Manufactured by Fairfield Graphics, Fairfield, Pennsylvania
Designed by M. M. Ahern
First Edition

Contents

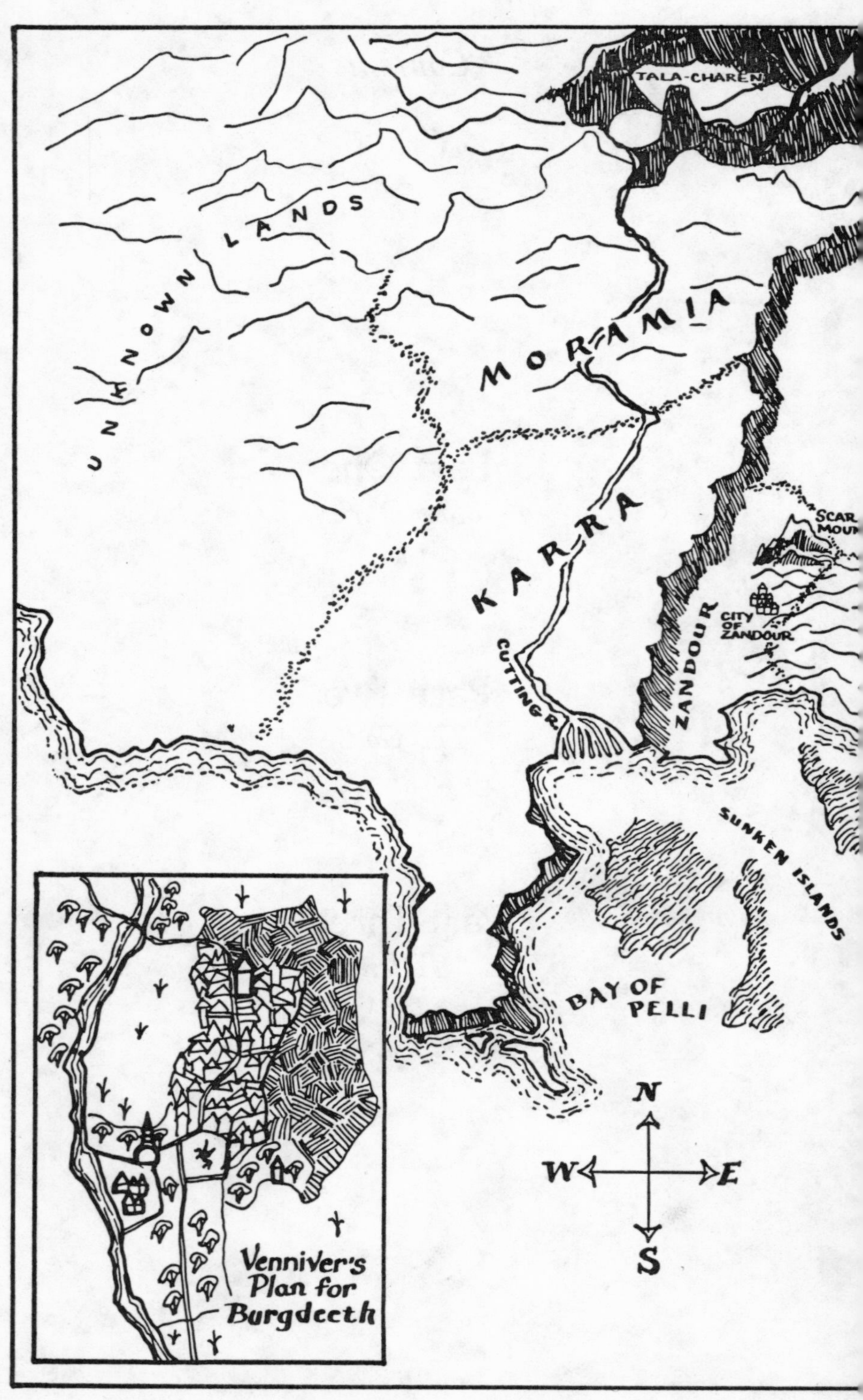
TALA-CHAREN
UNKNOWN LANDS
MORAMIA
KARRA
CUTTING R.
ZANDOUR
SCAR
CITY OF ZANDOUR
SUNKEN ISLANDS
BAY OF PELLI
N
W
E
S
Venniver's Plan for Burgdeeth

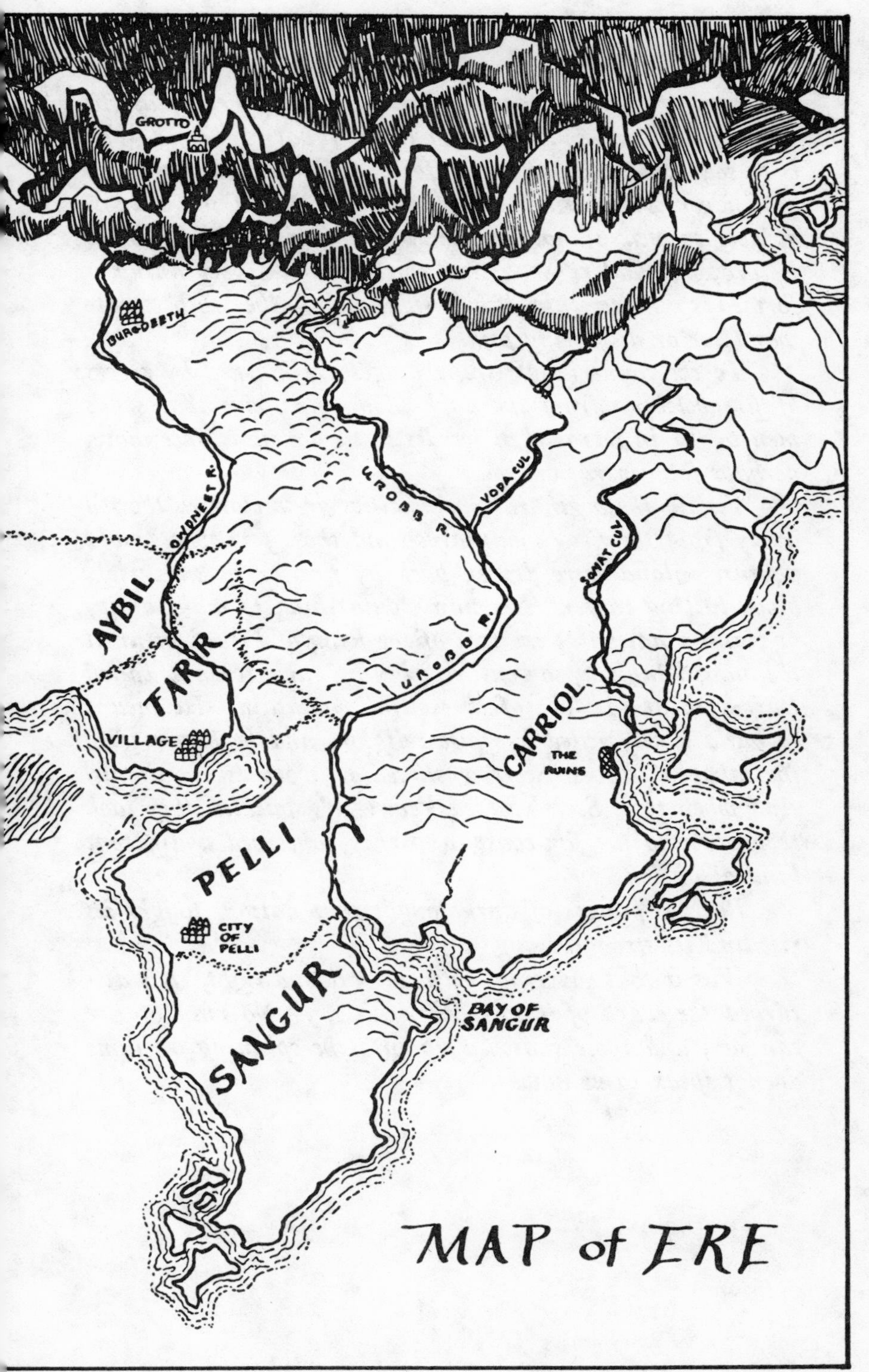
GROTTO
BURGDEETH
OWONEET R.
UROBB R.
VODA CUL
SOMAT CUL
AYBIL
FARR
VILLAGE
PELLI
CITY OF PELLI
CARRIOL
THE RUINS
SANGUR
BAY OF SANGUR
MAP of ERE

The ages of Time rise and move onward as neatly as the waves of the sea move. Or do they? What is *Time? Who is to say that each age moves forward in perfect symmetry and never is disturbed? Who is to say that Time cannot, as does the sea, tumble suddenly in a whirling rage so all is thrown asunder? So a time without end or beginning is formed spinning into itself, swallowing the unfortunate wanderer or displacing him.*

To the countries of Ere, the ages are marked by rivers of fire belching from the dark mountains, fire that sends men to flee in terror then recedes to lie dormant once more, perhaps for generations.

Yes, in the beginning men's cities grew close to the sea away from the fiery mountains, and those few who would venture inland were driven back by fire, or by maverick, blood-lusting raiders. No man would think to make a city or claim a nation at the foot of the Ring of Fire. Not until the man, Venniver, so ventured, laying out a town he called Burgdeeth at the foot of the wilful mountains. He meant to build a city ruled by false religion, and he began with the labor of slaves: Seers, enslaved to work like animals. And when those Seers escaped Venniver's shackles, they took themselves to the far coast, and they conceived a different kind of nation.

But the powers of dark fought that nation, fought its rise and its strengthening.

Was it that warring, between evil and light, that disturbed the warp of Time? Who can say? No man of Ere can say; and those snatched up into the spinning of Time do not speak to us now.

The Dark

Chapter One

THE MARE'S WINGS slashed and turned the wind. Ram clung to her back with effort, his fingers twisted in her mane to keep from falling, his blood spilling down across her shoulder. She lifted higher and the wind hammered at him; her wings tore light from the sun so it fractured around him, confusing him. He was hardly aware of the land below, blurred into a tapestry of green by her speed, was unaware of the river Urobb just beneath them and of the sea ahead. The bay and islands lay sun-washed, the towering stone ruins, but he did not heed them or the newly tilled farms, the herds of fat cattle and horses, did not see the carts going along the newly made roads toward the ruins to trade, was conscious only of pain, of sickness, of the raw pain of the sword wound in his side.

The bleeding increased. He loosed one hand from the mare's mane to explore the wound, then bent again, dizzy, hugging her neck to keep from falling. Only her mane torn by wind to slash across his face jerked him from unconsciousness. He pressed his arm tight to his side to staunch the blood.

The mare's wings spanned more than twenty feet, her dark eyes swept the sky and land constantly. Her golden coat caught the high, clear brilliance of the sun, her ears sharp forward and alert. She was no tame creature to come to a man's bidding, she had leaped from the sky of her own free will to lift Ram from the midst of battle, a dozen winged horses beside her sweeping down to lift the battered warriors from a fight that had turned to slaughter, so outnumbered were they; a battle they might have won had their Seer's powers not been crippled so the attack caught them unaware, the Herebian hordes surging through dense woods a hundred strong against their puny band.

The mare lifted higher now. Light filled her wings like a golden cloak surrounding Ram, light ever moving as she soared then angled down. The fields rolled beneath him sickeningly; he went dizzy again, and she warned him awake with cool equine concern; then she dropped suddenly and sharply to meet the cold sea wind, dove through the wind in swift flight supporting Ram with the strength of her will—then folded her wings in one liquid motion and stood poised and still on the rim of a stone balcony high up the sheer side of the temple of the gods.

Ram slipped down to the stone, his mind plunging toward blackness, and felt hands catch him. He saw a flash of gold as the mare leaped aloft, then went limp.

He woke swearing and flailing, thinking he was in battle, imagined men dying, could smell their blood. He was drenched in blood and sweat. He came fully awake at last, thrashing among the sweaty bedclothes. The wound in his side was a screaming pain. His bandage was soaked with blood. He felt hands lift his shoulders, saw white fingers around a cup. He swallowed the bitter drought gratefully, stared into Skeelie's thin face for an instant, then dropped into sleep again like a stone spinning down in deep water.

Skeelie stood over him scowling, shaken to see him hurt like this, grateful that he did not lie dead on some bloody battlefield. How many times had she stood so, wretched within herself at Ram's hurt? Ever since they were children so long ago in Burgdeeth, ever since that first time when he had been found unconscious from some strange attack, the great bruise on his head, the wolf tracks all around him and he left untouched by wolves. And the dead Pellian Seer lying near. She had nursed him like a baby then, a big boy of eight, near as big as she. And she had loved him then on that first day; but with a child's love, not as she loved him now. For all the good it did.

She was a tall girl. Her long, angled face, her dark hair pulled into a careless bun, her wrists protruding from her tunic sleeves made her seem gangling and awkward, though she was not. She stood praying to whatever there was to pray to that Ramad would not die. Half her life had been spent trying to heal the fool's wounds. Only, when they were children the wounds were not often so simple as those from arrow or sword; they had been wounds of a mind lashing out from darkness to contort Ram's spirit and nearly drive him mad. She touched his shoulder gently, laid her hand on his cheek, a thing she would hesitate to do if he were conscious. "You will *not* die, Ramad of wolves! You *can* not, you *must* not die!"

Above the sea wind she heard shouting voices then and turned from him to stand in the cavelike window to see flocking across the sky a dozen more winged horses. They swarmed down, the second wave of rescuers, diving through the sea wind to sweep onto the balconies below her, then stand quietly as their wounded were helped to dismount. She watched with clenched fists, sick at the slaughter their men had endured, and behind her Ram came awake suddenly shouting, "No gods! There are no gods!" Then came to himself and hunched up on one elbow wincing at the pain, stared straight at Skeelie, and growled, "Do you think I can lie here all day with nothing in my stomach, woman! Get me some food!" His red hair boiled over his forehead like the fires of the mountain itself.

"You can't eat solid food with a wound like that. I brought soup, there beside you on the shelf."

"I want meat! Get me some meat, Skeelie! I haven't eaten for two days!" He glared at the soup then pulled it closer and began to eat ravenously.

She went out, relieved at his stubborn strength, went down four stone flights to the great kitchen, among the clatter of women preparing poultices and herbs; she put cutlets to fry bloody rare and dished up some baked roots. Catching Dlos's eye where the older, wrinkled woman was hastily passing out bandages, she saw Dlos's concern for Ram, and grinning, put down her own concern. "He's cursing me and shouting for food." She saw Dlos's relief, then turned away. The kitchen was a hive of activity. She poured milk, then carried the mug and warm plate up to him as quickly as she could—and found him asleep again.

She sat beside his bed waiting for him to wake.

The first time she had ever brought him food, when they were children, she had fed him with a spoon like a baby. His red hair had been dyed black then, to disguise the Seer's skill that ran like fire in his veins. The swollen wound on his forehead had been meant, certainly, to kill him: his pursuers, if unable to take him captive, would surely have killed him. She could hear the sea crashing below, and a slash of afternoon sun caught across the foot of his bed; and all of an instant time seemed to flow together. The light-washed cave-room seemed one with the cobwebby storeroom where she had tended Ram so long ago, the two times seemed one time, the child Ram and the man he now was lay sprawled as one figure on the cot; she was as much a skinny frightened girl as she was a woman grown, no less afraid for Ram then than she was at this moment. Her hands shook. Then, seeing him wake, she reached for his plate, very practical suddenly, and began to cut his meat.

As his eyes lifted to her face, she felt the dark around them pressing at them, and she knew too well the presence of the dark Pellian Seers, their minds intruding unseen into the room. How she hated them: she sent hate back at them with a vehemence that at last drove the dark back until only a chill remained. She felt a brief fleeting satisfaction in that small power she had wielded; for her own skills were as nothing compared to Ramad's.

The dark had grown so strong. It was the same dark that had gripped and twisted Ram's mind when he was a child, only then it had been the Pellian Seer HarThass who had wielded it. Now, with HarThass dead, the strength of the dark had so increased under BroogArl's manipulations that it was a new and terrifying force over Ere, a force dedicated to Ram's destruction and to the destruction of all like him. The black Pellian's powers twisted and crippled the Seers of light now as never before. Made Ram's skills, the skills of the Carriolinian Seers, next to useless. An incredible force that blocked the Carriolinian skills so they could seldom, now, speak in silence even one with the other. They seldom, now, had foreknowledge of the fierce Herebian attacks as hordes swarmed over Carriol's borders to rape and burn and steal. Carriol's Seers were little more sensitive now to the forces around them than was any ordinary man. Only occasionally did BroogArl's powers abate for a few precious moments so their Sight was restored, like a sudden rent in the cloud-shrouded sky.

Ram ate ravenously. The wound seemed to make no difference to his hunger. She wished he had not bled so much; he was very pale. She took his empty plate at last and stood staring out again at the town, while behind her he stirred restlessly, thrashing the covers. Partly from the pain, she knew, but already wanting to get up. If he would just lie there sensibly and let the wound heal. . . . If she were closer to him, close in a different way, perhaps she could bully him into taking better care of himself. Perhaps. She scowled, annoyed at her own thoughts, and stared distractedly down at the street, where the wounded were being led and carried to their homes. The most critical would be lying in rooms in the tower where they could be doctored more easily and drugged against the pain. The stone sill beneath her hand was smooth from generations of use. This tower had seen so much, the lives of the gods who had dwelt here, the lives of the winged horses of Eresu and of those Seers who had come here for sanctuary in ages past: for in no age had the Seers of Ere been ignored by common men. Revered, yes. Worshipped and given rule, or driven out and killed as emissaries of the fire-spewing mountains, driven out so they came for sanctuary to the cities of the gods. Innocent Seers blamed for the fires of the earth, just as the gods had been blamed. And always there were evil Seers, too, revered by the ignorant and feared so it was easy for them to retain rule.

But never Seers left to themselves. In times past, only in the three cities of the gods had the gentle Seers found sanctuary from their evil brothers and from man's ignorance.

She caressed the smooth stone sill, and again a sense of Time slipping away gripped her so strongly she shivered. Suddenly she was very afraid, afraid for Ram—as if Time wanted suddenly to pull him into its wild vortex as it had done once when they were children. She turned to stare at him, stricken, was terrified in a way she could not understand. Where did this sudden sense come from of such danger? And, this sudden sense of someone reaching out to Ram with tenderness? Someone . . . . . She, Skeelie, was not a part of this.

Down on the street many of the wounded were beginning to come out again from doorways, their fresh bandages making pale slashes against sun-browned skin. They came toward the tower, came haltingly together beneath Ram's window, stared up at his portal, and their voices rose as one, supportive of him and vigorous, "*Ramad! We want Ramad!*" They shouted it over and over; then they began to sing Carriol's marching song, Carriol's song of victory, ". . . beyond the fire she stands unscathed, beyond the dark she towers . . ."

Their voices touched Skeelie unbearably. This handfull of men loving Ram so, loving Carriol so they must gather, wounded and half-sick, to sing of Carriol's victory—to reassure Ram of her victory. Skeelie heard Ram stir again, and turned expecting to see him rising painfully to come and stand beside her, to join with his troops.

But he had not risen. He lay looking across at her with an expression of utter defeat. "I can't, Skeelie. Tell them that I sleep."

She stared at him, shocked and chilled. Never had he refused to support his men, to cheer them when they were discouraged. Below her they sang out with lusty voices of defeating the Herebian, sang a song as old as Ere, as heartening as Ere's will was. For always had the Herebian bands laid waste the land, and always had men risen to defeat them. Renegade bands plundering and killing, and little villages and crofts fighting back. Though in times past the Herebian lust for cruelty had been simpler, for the dark had not ridden with them as it now did. In times past the Herebian bands had attacked the small settlements and infant nations, done their damage, been routed and weakened and moved on to attack elsewhere. Now all that was changed. Now the dark Seers led the Herebian hordes, and Carriol *must* defeat them, or die.

If ever Carriol should lie helpless before the Herebian tribes, the Pellian Seers would come forth to rule Carriol and to rule every nation of Ere. If Carriol and her Seers were defeated, it would be a simple matter indeed for the Pellians to manipulate the power of the small, corrupt families that dominated most of the other nations, manipulate the lesser, corrupt Seers there, and so devour those nations.

The singing voices rose to shout of victory; and when the last chorus died, its echo trembled against the ever present pounding of the sea. Ram's men stood looking upward waiting for him to appear.

"Tell them I sleep, Skeelie, can't you!"

"He sleeps—Ram is sleeping . . ."

"*Wake him! We want Ramad! Wake Ramad!*" Indomitable, hearty voices. Indomitable young men needing Ram now in their near defeat, in their aloneness and their repugnance of the dark that had stalked and crippled them so unbearably. Needing their leader now; but Ram only sighed and turned in his bed so his back was to the portal.

"I cannot wake him, he sleeps drugged for the pain . . ." She felt Ram's exhaustion, felt his inexplicable despair as if it were her own.

The silence of the men was sudden and complete. Skeelie stared down at them, sick at their defeat, and behind her Ram's voice was like death. "I can't, Skeelie. I think—I think I don't believe any more."

She turned to look at him.

"I'm tired. I'm tired of *all* of it. Do you understand that?"

"No, Ram. I don't understand that." She looked down at the men again, wanting to reassure them and not able. They began to sing simply and quietly, pouring their faith into words that might soothe the Ram's sleeping spirit. Ram did not stir at first. But after a few moments of the gentle song, the gentle men's voices, he could stand no more gentleness: he stirred angrily at last and threw the goathide back.

She supported him haltingly as he made his way toward the portal, then leaned heavily upon the stone sill. The men cheered wildly, laughed with pleasure at his presence, then went silent, waiting for him to speak. He was white as loess dust. He stood for a long moment, the blood oozing through his bandage. She thought he would speak of failure. She trembled for him, trembled for Carriol. How *could* he lose hope? He must not, they were not that close to defeat. These were Herebian bands, rabble they fought. *Rabble!* She watched him with rising dread of the words he would speak to his men as he leaned from the stone portal.

He shouted suddenly and so harshly that all of them startled. "*Yes victory! We are men of victory! We are a nation of victory!*" They cheered again and stood prouder as if a weight were lifted. Ram's voice was surer now. "The dark is ready for the grave! We will geld the dark, we will skewer the Pellians and bring such light into Ere as Ere has never seen!"

They went wild. "*Death to the dark ones! Death!*"

When at last they had released Ram, stronger in themselves, healed in themselves, Ram returned to his bed to lie with quick, shallow breathing, so very white. She sponged his forehead and smoothed his covers and could do nothing more. He lay quietly, staring up at her. "I have no idea in Urdd how we could skewer even one Pellian bastard, let alone pour light on what that son-of-Urdd BroogArl has wrought!" He closed his eyes and was silent for so long she thought he slept. Then he stared up at her again, his green eyes dark with more than physical pain, with a pain of the mind. "Something—there is something grown out of the Seer's hatred into a force of such strength, Skeelie. Almost like a creature with a will of its own, it is so powerful." He turned away then. But after a moment, "A power . . . a power that breathes and moves as one great lusting animal, Skeelie! That is the way I see the powers of the Seers of Pelli now."

She wanted to comfort him, wanted . . . but she could not comfort him. It would take another to comfort Ram. She stood washed with uncertainty. Could they defeat the Pellian Seers who ruled now the dark rabble hordes? Could they—or did Ram see too clearly a true vision of Carriol's defeat?

No. He was only tired, sick from the wound. Pain made him see only the grim side. She reached involuntarily to touch his cheek, then drew her hand back. She wanted to hold him, to soothe him in his pain of body and spirit, and she could not. Only another could do that.

And that other? He might never know her. Lost in another time and in another place, Ram might never know her. Skeelie turned away from him, furious at life, seeing once again that instant when she and Ram were swept out of time itself and Ram had looked, for one brief moment, onto the face of another and had been lost, then, to Skeelie forever.

When she looked back, he had risen and sat stiffly on the edge of his bed, seemed to be thinking all at once of something besides his pain and his own defeat. His look at her was pain of another kind. "Has there been no word of Jerthon? It is nine days since he rode to the north." He said it with a dry unhappiness that was like a worse defeat.

"He—no word. Nothing." A whole band out there fighting Kubalese troops and no message, no lone soldier riding back to bring news, no message sparking through Seers' minds to soothe Carriol's fears and to inform. Surely farms had been ravaged, captives taken, crops burned and farm animals driven across Carriol's western border into Kubalese lands.

Were there, then, no surviving soldiers? With the Seer's skills so destroyed by the dark, it was hard to know.

Had Jerthon . . . oh, Jerthon could *not* be dead. Her brother could not be dead.

"No message? No news, no sense of the battle, Skeelie? Can't you . . . ?"

"Nothing!" Skeelie snapped. "Nothing! Don't you think I've tried! Don't you think we all have!"

"But you—Tayba has the runestone. Hasn't she . . ." But then his frown turned suddenly from Skeelie toward the door, changed to a look of concern, and Skeelie turned to look.

Tayba stood there, handsome even in faded coarsespun, but her dark hair wild, her cheeks pale. There was fear in her expression and something of guilt. Ram rose at once, catching his breath at the pain, and went to his mother's side. "What is it? You . . ."

"Joheth Browden brought a woman and two children in from his little farm north of Folkstone." Her voice was shaking. "Brought them in the wagon. They—they were nearly starved and they—they have been mistreated. They escaped from the Kubalese, but before—before that they . . ." She seemed nearly unable to speak. "Before that, Ram—they escaped from Burgdeeth." She stopped, was almost in tears. Her dark hair lay tangled across Ram's arm. She swallowed. "Those little girls saw their nine-year-old sister burned to death. Burned, Ram! Burned in Venniver's fire! In Venniver's cursed ceremonial fire!" She pushed her face against Ram's shoulder so her voice came muffled. "It has come, Ram. A child has been burned alive. The thing we dreaded . . ."

Skeelie stared at them, her fists clenched, feeling Tayba's awful dismay, and Tayba's shame. Her own emotions were so confusing and unclear.

Tayba had been Venniver's woman, in Burgdeeth. Tayba had nearly killed Ram, her own son, and nearly killed Skeelie's brother Jerthon, too, with her treachery.

If she had behaved differently, Venniver would be dead now and there would be no ceremonial fires, no children dying. Burgdeeth would be free and not ruled by a false religion. Tayba was suffering all of it now again, all the guilt and terror from those days, flooding out. "We thought to stop it in time," Tayba whispered. "And we have not. A child has burned. A child—a Seeing child . . ."

Ram spoke at last, his voice strangely cold. "We have always known it, Mamen. We have always known it would come." And then, bitterly, "We did not know our Seers would be blinded and unable to know when it was to happen."

Skeelie stood watching them dumbly, then at last she pushed by them out of the room and went down the twisting stone flights to the kitchen.

Chapter Two

In the kitchen the open fire had just been fed, its flames blazed up, lighting the faces of the three frightened refugees clustered around it: a tall woman, a girl perhaps thirteen, and a very little girl who was being bathed by Dlos in the wooden tub. The woman was half-undressed and washing herself in some private ritual as if to wash away all that had been done to her. A dozen Carriolinian women were bustling about preparing food, bringing clean clothes. Skeelie knelt by the tub and took the little girl from Dlos as the old woman fetched her out. The child was covered with sores. Skeelie dried her, then began to dress her. "What is your name? Can you tell me your name?" The child would not speak. Her lank brown hair was dark from the tub.

"She is Ama," said her older sister. "I am Merden." Merden had a long, thin face and lank hair like her little sister. They both looked remarkably like their mother. Little Ama spoke then, softly against Skeelie's shoulder. "Our sister Chanet is dead in the fire. *Why* is Chanet dead? *Why did the Landmaster burn her?*"

The older girl touched her little sister's shoulder, stared unseeing at Skeelie with an expression that brought goose bumps. "Chanet was only . . . she was nine years old."

When Ram came to stand in the doorway, the tall young woman glanced at him, then carelessly pulled clothes around her as if she had been exposed so often to male eyes that another pair made little difference. As if her ablutions were more immediate than modesty. Ram turned away until she was dressed, then came to speak to her. Skeelie watched him in silence. He'd never begin to heal if he didn't stay in bed, he had no more business coming down here—no more sense than a chidrack sometimes. She stared pointedly at his bloody bandages. He ignored her.

Mawn Paula told Ram her story quickly and almost without expression, as if she held her emotions very taut within herself, afraid to let them go. She and her three little girls had been kneeling in temple when, in the middle of the ceremony, Venniver rose from the dais and came down among the benches. Without warning he reached across Ama and Merden and pulled Chanet from her seat, jerked her into the aisle and stood scowling down at her, his black beard bristling, his cold blue eyes piercing in their study of the child. The temple had been silent. Those in front had glanced behind them uneasily then stared forward again. Mawn had remained quiet, terrified for the child, fearful that the least motion, the least whisper from her would jeopardize Chanet further. After a long scrutiny, Venniver had forced the child before him up the aisle to the dais. Mawn had remained with great effort in her place. She had not let herself believe the truth, even then, that Venniver knew Chanet for a Seer, that he meant to kill her, to sacrifice her on the altar of fire, could not let herself believe it. It was only when Venniver forced Chanet with brutal blows to confess to Seer's skills, that Mawn must believe. And even then she had sat frozen, terrified, as Venniver made the child climb the steps to the top of the dais.

Chapter Two

When Venniver began to tie Chanet to the steel stake, Mawn had screamed and leaped up, had run to stop him, fighting the red-robed Deacons. They tried to hold her as she bit and scratched and hit out at them, finally they had her in a grip she could not break. Ama and Merden had fought fiercely, but at last all three were held immobile and forced to remain still as nine-year-old Chanet was burned to death in the flames of Venniver's ceremonial fire as appeasement to the gods.

Skeelie heard the story, sick with revulsion. A child burned to death as appeasement. Appeasement to the gods. She lifted her eyes to Ram to see her hatred of Venniver reflected in his face, see her pain reflected there.

Mawn and the two girls had escaped Burgdeeth late at night while the guards sat drinking in the Hall. They slipped down into the tunnel as soon as it was dark, the secret tunnel that no one but a Seer could know of. Then they left the tunnel again well after midnight to make their way out of Burgdeeth in the sleeping, silent hours. They took little with them but some vegetables hastily pulled from the gardens and a waterskin they had found in the tunnel.

Ram listened intently to this, and Skeelie nearly wept, so thankful was she now for the painful years her brother Jerthon had spent digging that tunnel secretly beneath Venniver's very nose while he was held as Venniver's slave.

"And then you were captured by the Kubalese?" Ram said.

"Yes, in the hills," Mawn said. "We were digging roots."

"It must have been bad."

"Yes. It was bad."

"Will you tell me what the Kubalese stockade is like? Will you tell me as much as you can about their camp?"

"The stockade is like houses for chidrack, thick boards with space between and the roof is the same so rain comes in. The soldiers watch you undress, do—do everything. The boards are far too thick to break without tools. The herd animals are in pens close by. You are fed once a day on gruel and stale water. We were . . . we were sick much of the time. The guards . . . they didn't open the gate, they just shoved the food through. A girl . . . she was the leader's daughter, though he treats her badly. She slipped extra food to us and fresh water. She helped us to escape. Ama and Merden, when we were away, both knew that she was beaten for what she did."

"It was," Merden said, "as if the thing that kept us from Seeing opened out all at once and we could See. All—all of a sudden. We—we didn't want to see that. We didn't want to see her father beat her."

Ram stared at her. Her voice seemed to fuzz so he could barely understand her. He was growing weak, the room swam, seemed hazy around him. The pain and bleeding were worse. "Were you—were you the only captives?"

She hesitated at his obvious discomfort, then continued. "There were many captives. When—when Telien freed us she had the key for only a minute, when her father left it by the water trough as he ran to catch a loose horse. He had been—in our pen, making . . . been in our pen. Telien unlocked the lock then slipped it round so it looked locked. She whispered for us to wait until dark. She put the key back before he returned, and there was no time to free the others.

"We got out after dark and went up into the hills, then we came south and east until we saw the little settlements and knew we must be in Carriol."

The mention of the girl Telien made a disquiet in Skeelie, though she could not think why. She had never heard of Telien, knew nothing of such a girl. But her uneven Seer's sense reached out now to concern itself with this girl so suddenly and with such distress that Skeelie trembled. She did not understand what she felt, knew only that she was suddenly and inexplicably uneasy.

Merden turned from combing her little sister's hair. "Telien—Telien told us about Carriol." She stared at Ram. "Telien spoke of you, of Ramad of the wolves . . ."

Skeelie stiffened.

Merden smiled, a faint, uncertain smile. "Telien said that you would care for us, that we could make a new life here, that all who want freedom can. She spoke of the leader Jerthon, too, and of a world—a world very different from what we have known."

Skeelie hardly heard the child for the unease and pounding in her heart. Yet she had no reason to feel anything for a girl from Kubal. What was the matter with her? She was almost physically sick with the sense of the girl.

Merden said quietly, "Telien said the leaders of Carriol were close to the gods. That you—that you have more powers than we do. That maybe you will be able to stop the killing in Burgdeeth." She looked at Ram with such trust that he wanted to turn from her—or shout at her. Mawn, seeing his look, whispered diffidently, "Telien told us you command—command the great wolves that live in the Ring of Fire."

"No one . . ." Ram said, wincing, "No one commands the great wolves. They—they are my friends. My brothers."

Skeelie said uneasily, angrily, "If a girl of Kubal knows such things, surely she is a Seer." What was wrong with her, why *was* she bristling so?

"No," Mawn said, "Telien is not a Seer. She learned what she knows of Carriol, of you, from the other captives. From Carriol's settlers taken captive. They say Carriol is the only place of freedom in all of Ere."

Later, when Ram had allowed himself to be helped upstairs by two of his men coming in to raid the larder, Skeelie asked Merden the question that would not let her be. "What is she like? What is this Telien like?" And when Merden looked back at her, that serious, thin, child's face quietly reflecting, then described Telien, Skeelie could not admit to herself the terrible sudden shock that gripped her.

"Telien has pale, long hair. She is slight and she—she is beautiful."

Skeelie stared, stricken. "And—and her eyes are green, are they not? Green eyes like the sea."

"Yes. That is Telien." Merden watched Skeelie, puzzling. She said nothing more. Perhaps she saw in Skeelie's face, heard in her questions, more than Skeelie intended to show.

And Skeelie stood remembering bitterly and clearly that moment when she and Ram had, as children, stood inside the mountain Tala-charen, had felt time warp, had seen those ghostly figures appear suddenly out of time, seen the pale-haired, green-eyed girl stare at Ram with such eager recognition, with a terrible longing as if she would cross the chasm of time to Ram or die.

Was Telien that girl? Was she here now, in Ram's own time? But *this* time had been only a dim, unformed future when Ram was eight. *This* time had not yet happened. How could— She broke off her thoughts, her head spinning.

He had never forgotten that girl. Never. Though he had never once spoken of her.

Was Telien that girl? Had she lived in *this* time? Had she traveled backward in Time to the long ago day when Ram was nine? Was she here in this time, and would Ram find her? Skeelie turned away. Had the thing that she dreaded so long at last come to pass? She went from the kitchen in silence.

She went down through the town to the stables, got a horse, and rode out along the sea at a high, fast gallop that left her horse spent, and at last, left her a little easier in herself. If this were Ram's love, come to claim him, then she must learn to live with it just as she had lived with the knowledge that one day it would surely happen.

IT WAS not until four days later, in the middle of the simple worship ceremony in the citadel, that Skeelie's brother Jerthon returned from the battle in the north, coming quickly into citadel in his sweaty fighting leathers. A ripple of welcome went through the citadel, through the singing choir, and Skeelie wanted to run to him. She found it hard to keep singing as he sat down heavily in the back row next to Ram. Jerthon leaned against the stone wall as if he were very tired, stared up at the light-washed ceiling, and seemed to listen to the hush of the sea, to listen in sudden peace to the choir's rising voices.

The citadel was the largest hall in the honeycombed natural stone tower that had once been the city of the gods. Here in the citadel the winged gods and the winged horses of Eresu had come together for companionship; a meeting place, a place of solace and joy where the outcast Seers had come too, in gentle friendship. A place where the moving light, cast across the ceiling by the ever-rolling sea, seemed to hold sacred meaning; and the cresting sea made a gentle thunder like a constant heartbeat. Skeelie saw Jerthon lift his chin in that familiar sigh, then turn to stare at Ram, saw Ram speak.

Ram stared at Jerthon for a long solemn moment, then grinned. Jerthon's appearance in citadel so suddenly was like the sun coming out. Not dead, not lying wounded in some field, but strolling nonchalantly into citadel in the middle of service. Ram wanted to shout and throw his arms around Jerthon. He cuffed him lightly. "Your face is dirty. You could do with a bath. Was it bad in the north?"

"Yes, bad." There was a deep cut across Jerthon's chin and neck. His red hair, darker than Ram's, was pale with chalky dust. He was quiet as usual, contemplative. Had learned to be, with half his life spent in slavery to the tyrant Venniver. Had learned not to be hot-headed as Ram still was sometimes. Jerthon's voice showed the strain of the last days. "We lost near twenty men, lost horses. The Kubalese took captives heavy in Blackcob, took men, women and children—took most of the horses roped together, and the captives made to run before them." His jaw muscles were tight, his eyes hard. "We have relied too long on the skills of Seeing, Ram, and now we are crippled without them. Our scouts saw too little, our border guards did not sense the Herebian scouts or the Herebian bands slipping in. Oh, we routed those that didn't go riding off with captives and stolen horses before we could rally ourselves. They set on us in waves, there must have been bands from half a dozen Herebian strongholds. Raiders creeping out like rats to snatch and kill and disappear. And something—" Jerthon stared at Ram with a barely veiled slash of fear in his eyes. "Something rides with them, Ram. Something more than the dark we know, something . . . dense. Like an impossible weight on your mind so the Seeing is torn from you and your very sanity near torn from you."

"Yes. I know that feeling. I had it too. We all did."

"We must never again—never—allow our senses to be so dulled by reliance on Seeing alone. We must guard against that. We must train against it."

"Yes. I know we must."

Jerthon pushed back a lock of red hair so violently that a cloud of the white dust rose to drift in motes on the still citadel air. "I think the hordes will not march here, though I've given orders for double guard and for mounts kept ready." He grew silent, as if he were drawn away. The choir's voices rose to lilt along the ceiling like the wash of sea light.

". . . faith then, faith in men then, faith to do then, faith to be . . ." rising higher and higher, Skeelie's voice clearly discernible now; but now that song seemed a joke in the face of the murder Jerthon had witnessed.

Ram hardly heard the voices that rang across the cave. He sat looking inward at his own failure. For if they had the whole runestone of Eresu in their possession, they could easily defeat the dark. That round jade sphere, which he had held in his hands, carried power enough to defeat every evil Seer in Ere.

He had held it, seen it shatter asunder, seen its shards disappear from his open palm—seen those shards vanish out of Time into the hands of others, mysterious figures come out of Time in that instant.

He had returned to Jerthon with one small shard of jade. That shard, that bit of the runestone, was now the only force beyond their own Seer's skills with which they could battle the dark.

That moment would burn forever in his mind. He had felt the earth rock, felt Time warp and come together, was shaken by thunder as Time spun to become a vortex out of Time. He had stood helplessly as the stone turned white hot and shattered in his hands. And something of himself had gone then, too. He had known, since that time, an oppressive loss, a loss he did not really understand.

He and Skeelie had come down out of the mountain Tala-charen the next morning to make their way across unknown valleys to meet Jerthon and Tayba, meet all those who had escaped from Burgdeeth and Venniver's enslavement.

He had placed the jade shard in Jerthon's hand, and

Jerthon had looked down at him—a tall, red-headed Seer staring down at a nine-year-old boy who had so recently seen his dreams, his hope for Ere, shatter. Jerthon had read the two runes inscribed on the jade; "*Eternal—will sing,*" then had looked hard at Ram. "Did it sing, Ram?"

"If you call thunder a song. But where—the other parts . . . ?"

"It went into Time, and that is all we can know. Now, in each age from which those Children came, Time will warp again, once, in the same way."

Ram stared at the choir unseeing, shutting their voices from his mind. Could he have prevented the shattering of the stone? And if he had prevented it, what would have happened differently these past twelve years?

They had begun their journey that morning from the wild mountain lands above Burgdeeth to Carriol, and to Jerthon's home. Carriol then was a collection of small crofts and farms, of peaceful men and women holding their freedom stubbornly against the ever-threatening Herebian bands. Joyful, vigorous men and women ready always to battle for their hard-won freedom.

Now, twelve years later, Carriol was a nation. With the easy cooperation between the Carriolinian Seers and those who came from slavery in Burgdeeth, with an easy-open council, they had welded Carriol into a strong, cohesive country. The few crofts at the foot of the ruins had grown into a town. The ready bands that had ridden to defend neighbors' lands had grown into four fierce, well-disciplined battalions of fighting men backed by women who were equally skillful at arms.

And as Carriol grew stronger, the wrath of the Pellian Seers had grown. The Pellian, BroogArl, had drawn the evil Seers of all nations into an increasingly malevolent unity directed toward Carriol, a unity of dark that breathed hate poisonous as vipers upon the air of that rising free land, rose in increasing anger that Carriol was sanctuary where men could come in need to escape the evils of the dark Seers, and that Carriol was becoming too strong to attack.

All the political intrigue and manipulating among small-minded leaders in other countries that so increased the lack of freedom of an unwitting populace, all the atrocities done to common men for the pleasure and diversion of those leaders as their evil lust began to feed on itself—all of this was threatened if fearful serfs could escape to Carriol and be protected there.

There had been a great, concerted effort by Ere's dark Seers to bring all the nations but Carriol under one iron-gloved rule, one dark entity that could devour Carriol: a war-hungry giant that could crush her. The Seers of Carriol had so far prevented that, with the help of the runestone. But if they had had the whole stone, had held that great power, what more could they have done?

Surely they would have prevented—made impossible—the burning of a Seeing child in Venniver's fires.

Ram glanced at Jerthon and found him scowling. He touched Jerthon's arm, seeking for some silent contact, but caught only a fleeting sense of unease, nothing more.

Jerthon loosed his leather tunic, looked as if he would like to pull off his boots. "Lieutenant Prail told me the winged ones pulled you out of that bloody trap in the south." He stared at Ram. "The horses of Eresu did not come near us, we did not see them or feel their presence. It seems to me something goes on with them, but I can't make out what—as if there is fear among them. I think that evil stalks the winged ones just as evil stalks us. Only once did we hear their voices in our minds for a moment—beseeching voices laced with fear. Then the silence returned."

Ram shifted, easing the strain on his wound. It itched

abominably now that it had started to heal. "The golden mare who brought me had a sadness about her. Also, Jerthon, something is amiss with them, as well as with the world of men."

Jerthon stared across the citadel to where Skeelie stood tall in the choir, the sun striking her robe. His sister sang as if her whole soul were lifted and bouyed by the music. He said, with more heart, "I ride in a few hours to rescue the captives taken in the north; I came back only to get up fresh mounts and more men. Arben's battalion rides north of Blackcob now. They will wait for us just below the mountains, to come on the Kubalese camp from high ground. I ride south, and those few men left in Blackcob ride out direct over the hills eastward. We will come upon Kubal from three sides. But there . . . I think there is someone in the Kubalese camp who is in sympathy with us. I had only a fleeting feel of it, but perhaps he can help us if we can summon the power to reach him. It would be good to have a spy inside to loose horses, cut saddle bands and otherwise cripple the Kubalese.

Ram felt a strange sense stir him, an unfamiliar excitement. He paused, feeling outward, but could make nothing of it; and it was gone so quickly. He brought himself back to Jerthon. "Yes—perhaps I know of whom you speak." What was this pounding of his pulse? "Perhaps I know, for we have had news of Kubal . . ." And the very word *Kubal* seemed to speak to him in some way; but he could make nothing of it. He reached out, tried to sense whatever it was, and could not, frowned, irritated at himself. "There are captives from Kubal come three days ago, brought in by wagon from Folkstone. They escaped from Burgdeeth after a child was—burned to death in Venniver's sacrificial flames."

"You . . ." Jerthon stared at him. "It has begun, then. The burning has begun."

"Yes. What we feared has begun." Ram looked away toward the portal. This defeat, on top all the rest, was nearly unbearable. Well, it must be told. Jerthon waited to hear. He sighed, continued.

"The mother and the child's two sisters escaped through the tunnel, then later were captured by the Kubalese as they dug roots in the hills. They were helped to escape Kubal by a young girl—the Kubalese leader's daughter, they said." And again that strange excitement swept him, a sharp sense of anticipation. "The girl is Ag-Wurt's daughter, but they said she brought extra food and water to them, helped them. Perhaps it is she you touched, perhaps she . . ." Why did the very mention of the girl unnerve him? "If she could help us . . ."

"Perhaps. We can try." Jerthon sat hunched, scowling. Then at last, "The burning of a child should never have occurred. We have waited too long. Curse the Pellian Seers, curse the blindness they put on us!"

Ram shifted, easing his wound. "I ride tonight to carry out the plan we made long ago. I ride for Eresu to speak with the gods, to beg their help in stopping Venniver."

Jerthon stared at him. "With that wound? You can't ride alone with that wound. *We* will go this night."

"You are committed to meet Arben."

"There are lieutenants who can—"

Ram shook his head. "It would be foolish for us to be together. And the runestone . . ."

"Tayba will guard the runestone well and use it if it is needed."

"*Do* you trust my mother, Jerthon, even yet? After her treachery against you in Burgdeeth?"

Jerthon gave him a look that withered him. "That was twelve years back, lad! She has proven—since that time—her quality. You know I trust her—more than trust her. And she . . . Tayba has the most skill with the stone.

A traitor, Ram—a traitor turned to love the cause he betrayed is often the steadiest of all." He paused as the choir's voices rose . . .

> "They touch the star. The force of Waytheer
> Brings us closer, gods and men.
> Ynell's true Children never waver,
> Though falter, Seers dark with lusting,
> Falter you."

The voices echoed against the cadance of the pounding sea. Jerthon said quietly, "What makes us really believe the gods will help us in curbing Venniver's lust for the burning of children?"

". . . Falter, Seers dark with lusting, *Falter you* . . ."

"The gods *must* help. Even if they have never helped men except to offer sanctuary, even if their beliefs say that to help is to tamper with the natural conditions of men, still this time, Jerthon, they must! I will—somehow I will—see that they do. If—if they are truly gods they . . ."

"I have no patience with that old discussion!" Jerthon wiped dust from his cheek with the back of his hand. "It means nothing. Anyway it makes no difference, true gods or not, they are capable of helping—if they will."

". . . Falter, Seers dark with lusting, *Falter you* . . ."

Jerthon looked at him for a long moment. "It is up to you, then, Ramad of wolves."

The last stanza died echoing inside the citadel, the last tones rising and lingering against the pounding heartbeat of the sea. Ram and Jerthon rose as one and left the citadel. Skeelie stared after them and knew from the look of them they would both be off on some wild business, and bit her lip in anger. Damn the Pellian Seers! Damn this ugly, useless, harassing, small-minded, terrifying war!

Chapter Three

Ram rode out for Blackcob well before dusk. As he left the ruins, he turned in the saddle and saw Skeelie standing in a portal watching him. He waved, but wished she were not compelled to see him ride out, compelled to worry over him. She had sat with him while he ate an early meal, nagged him about his wound, as had Tayba. He turned his back on the ruins and made his way through the village. The low sun behind the stone houses made the thatched roofs shine, sent deep shadows across the cobbles. His horses' hooves struck sharp staccato as he exchanged greetings with men and women coming in from work, from the drilling field. He could smell suppers cooking. Children flocked around his two horses then stormed away like leaves blown. He left the town at last to pass occasional farms along the sea cliff, then soon the cliff was empty of all but the sweeping grass, the wind salt and harsh. Waves pounded up the side of the cliff bouncing spray into his face. He relished the solitude, needed this solitude to heal the sense of defeat that would not leave him, the sense of mounting disaster. The sense of wasted lives. They had lost some good men at Folkstone. He would be a long time forgetting it.

And the attacks kept coming. Not a large, full-scale battle, but small, bedeviling attacks first in one place, then another, harassing the farmers and herders, delaying what should have been the joyful, disorderly growth of the new country; destroying crops, stealing livestock . . .

Yes, and that was just what the Seer BroogArl intended. Delay and harassment, the wasting of Carriol's resources, the disrupting of her peaceful pursuits, of building new craftsmen's shops, of fencing rich pasture, breaking new farmland. All lay untended, interrupted as Carriol's settlers went off to defend the land—and perhaps to die. Such harassment did BroogArl's work most effectively. If it lasted long enough, Ram wondered reluctantly, *could* the Pellian Seers conquer Carriol?

And something else kept nudging him, a feeling of urgency that puzzled him. His senses seemed infected by it. As if, ahead, lay not only his mission to the gods, to the valley of Eresu, but something else—something beckoning. The very air around him seemed fresh with anticipation, the wind sharper, even the sea meadows seemed brighter in spite of his sickness at the recent battle, in spite of his mourning of friends. He had no idea what made such a feeling, but the sense of anticipation refused to leave him, and the ride along the coast seemed as perfect as the songs in citadel, rich and full of subleties, glorious with the powers of sea and wind.

He must be growing foolish; this must be some twisting of his mind grown out of his relief at being still alive after battle. Some wild reverence for life so nearly lost.

Even when the pack mare grew edgy, snorting and pulling back, he was more amused than disturbed. He spoke only gently to his own mount when he started to sidestep and stare at emptiness. The waning day was clear as a jewel; there was nothing to disturb them.

They settled at last and Ram, lulled by the steady rhythm of the sea, thought with pleasure of the two-year-old colts that would be ready soon for breaking. Fine colts, near the finest yet of the new breed he and Jerthon had taken so much time with. Well-made, eager animals, sensible in battle—not like these two, gaping at nothing. Colts that would one day sire a line of the finest horses in Ere, quick, short-coupled horses, handy in battle and fast and brave in attack.

He left the sea cliffs with reluctance to head inland, down through low-lying fog into the marsh cut by the river Somat Cul as it flowed south to meet the sea. The river was flanked here by coppery reeds, the air very still. Even the suck of hooves was silenced by the press of fog. The marsh smelled of decaying life and of new growth. Ahead, the fog thickened into a mass as heavy as a wall. As he approached it, the pack mare snorted and plunged wildly, and his mount went spraddle-legged, staring. A hushing sigh came from the mass of fog, then all at once, where the fog was thickest, a shape began to form.

It was tall, seemed to swell in size until it loomed above him. Was it . . . *was it winged? A winged figure?* But it was too large to be a horse of Eresu. Was that a human torso rising between the great shadows of its wings? *Not a god!*

It was utterly silent, did not speak into his mind as a god would. As the fog thickened further, it all but vanished, yet the frightened horses plunged and fought him so wildly it was all he could do to keep the frantic mare from pulling away.

The figure darkened again, came clearer. Then it spoke to him. "Ramad! You are Ramad!" Its voice was hollow, void of expression or of kindness. And it spoke aloud, not in a god's thought-language. He swallowed, waited in silence, clutching his sword and knowing a sword was useless.

"You are Ramad of wolves, are you not! Answer me, Seer!"

Ram did not answer, did not move.

"Afraid to speak, cowardly Seer? Well hear me then! You pursue an unworthy mission, Ramad of wolves! You ride sniveling like a baby to whimper before gods! Ignorant mortal, would you lay the troubles of *men* before *gods* to solve?" Then the creature laughed, a terrifying, rasping thunder that echoed through the fog.

Ram fought it with his mind, tried with Seer's powers to reduce it to the fog from which it must have formed, fought uselessly, all his skills unable to turn aside the dark being. It swelled larger, and the mist around it seethed, and it screamed at him, "Turn back, Seer! Turn back from your precarious quest lest you destroy the very cause you so covet!"

Suddenly the horses became strangely still. The creature shifted, and Ram felt himself grow dizzy. In spite of the fear that threatened to engulf him, he made his voice thunder in return. "If you give me honest words, show yourself!" *Did* he see the turn of a horse's body, a man's torso rising from its withers? All was so unclear, constantly changing. *Was* this a god with some enmity he had never imagined a god to have? Yet the sense that emanated from the mist was not godlike, was forbidding and cold. "If you speak truly," Ram challenged again, "show yourself to me!"

It's laugh was terrible. But it began to fade until soon its gigantic form was only a wash of dark. The mist thinned and receded. Coppery reeds showed through. And there was, suddenly, nothing before him. Only the river, reflecting Ere's rising moons. Farther upriver, a heron screamed.

Ram sat staring at the marsh where the thing had risen. His wound throbbed. He felt spent, dead of spirit suddenly. When at last he started on again the horses walked as heavily as if they had already traveled the night's distance. Ram felt as a child feels after a time of fever—as he had felt when he was small and his mind had been swept away during sleep into the dark Pellian caves by the Seer HarThass, possessed there by HarThass so he had battled for his life, was left so weak and listless afterward he hardly cared for life. Now he felt the same, weak, without volition. Without purpose. Too sharply he remembered HarThass's lurid mind and inner worlds, which had spun him away from the living so he had been able to cling only tenuously to any strength within himself. Never, since that time, had he known complete freedom from the dark harassment of the Pellian Seers: a curse that, perhaps, had been welded into the fabric of reality generations before his birth, when a dark Seer lay dying in the caves of Zandour, predicting his birth, predicting his destiny.

Well enough he knew, from the teaching of Seers greater than he, from the words of the Luff'Eresi themselves in visions and written on the walls of a far cave among the Ring of Fire, that no man's destiny was fixed. That no man danced to a pattern like a puppet on an invisible string. How had that long-dead Seer known then, that Ram would be born, that Ram would carry the blood of the cult of wolves? Had that Seer, before he died, been swept ahead on the living warp of Time to touch the fabric of Ram's birth and life? He must have done; for others had known his words, though he spoke them quite alone in the cave of the wolf cult that would become his tomb:

A bastard child will be born and he will rule the wolves as no Seer before him has done. A bastard child fathered by a Pellian bearing the last blood of the wolf cult. My blood! My blood seeping down generations hence from some bastard I *sired and do not even know exists. A child born of a girl with the blood of Seers in her veins. A child that will go among the great wolves of the high mountains where the lakes are made of fire . . .*

In the throes of death, had that Seer swung into the fulcrum of Time for his vision, just as Ram and Skeelie had stood in that fulcrum when the runestone of Eresu split?

Always the memory of that prophesy, repeated to him out of the dark mind of the Seer HarThass, left him agape with wonder, weak with a knowledge of the incredible—yet he, too, had ridden the warp of Time, when he stood inside the mountain Tala-charen.

And his own experience had left him restless, with a fierce need that he could never make come clear. As if he were not whole suddenly, as if something had been left behind there in that spinning, thundering, echoing warp of Time; something that was terribly a part of him.

When he came at last out of the marsh where the river foamed over rocks, he was among scattered farms, fields of whitebarley and mawzee, fat grazing animals lifting their heads to watch him pass. A horse nickered, but Ram's horses did not return the greeting, remained quiet and subdued. The sun had dropped behind hills, leaving a pale orange wash preceeding nightfall. The council would be meeting now in citadel, would sit around the meeting table, the jade runestone gleaming in the center. Outside the portal, the thin moons would rise. The council would lay careful plans for the protection of Carriol—plans perhaps destined to go awry, he thought bitterly. And they would discuss Jerthon's attack on Kubal. Jerthon, riding out again so soon to battle. Jerthon who was more father to Ram than a real father could have been: Seer, teacher of Seer's powers, his mentor since the days Ram first turned to him for protection from the dark Pellian. Jerthon, whom his mother loved but would not marry because of the guilt she carried and refused to put aside.

Ram wished she would come to her senses. She need feel no guilt, she had proven that. He wished she would marry Jerthon and be done with this stupidity. Eresu knew, Jerthon wanted her. It was Jerthon who had drawn forth, from Tayba's wilful spirit, power undreamed; more power even than Ram had imagined his mother possessed. It was Jerthon who had taught her to use that power, who had loved her for the strengths he saw despite her weaknesses.

And he had seen her look at Jerthon. He knew what she felt for him. Yet she wouldn't marry him, felt she alone was responsible for their partial defeat in Burgdeeth, for having to leave the town in Venniver's hands; felt now, Ram knew, a burning guilt that a child had burned in Venniver's fires. Believed that without her near-betrayal, her partial betrayal, Burgdeeth would now stand as a free city and safe for Seers.

And she was, Ram knew, very likely right. Well, but you could not carry guilt all your life. She had made amends, made a new life; she was a fierce, willing fighter for what Jerthon and all of them stood for. Why in Urdd didn't she marry Jerthon and give him, and herself, some happiness.

THE COOL LIGHT of evening washed the citadel. The sea roared like a large, slow animal, and wind hushed through the portals smelling sharply of salt and kelp. Tayba pulled her red cloak lightly around her shoulders and stared almost transfixed at the runestone: powerful talisman, shard of deep green jade, jagged where it had split away from the whole sphere, smooth and rounded at the large end and marked with incomplete runes. A stone that, if it had not been for her lusting, stupid hungers, might lie here whole now, round, perfect and immensely more powerful—though even this shattered shard could concentrate and strengthen the powers of the Carriolinian Seers. Only . . . not enough. Not enough power to battle the Pellian Seers in their new, incredible force.

And this jagged bit of jade was a symbol, too, of the

frightening powers Tayba found within herself and which she had not, even yet, learned to deal with easily; though she tried. With Jerthon's help, she tried.

There sat at the council table, eight of Carriol's fifteen Seers. Five of that eight had come to Carriol from Burgdeeth twelve years ago after freeing themselves from Venniver's slave cell. They were Tayba; Jerthon, who sat with his back to the portal, the fading light casting a halo around his red hair; his sister Skeelie, her wrists protruding from her tunic as usual, her skewered hair awry, her dark eyes turned to some inward pain as she tried without success to See Ramad on his lonely journey—none of their skills were worth a spoon of spit since the dark Seers had learned to master such cold, impregnable force.

The fourth of the group was Drudd. He sat as far from Tayba as he could manage. Always he avoided her as deliberately as he had done in Burgdeeth. Then, he had had reason to do so. The short stocky forgeman, who had worked by Jerthon's side to forge the great bronze statue they had left behind them in Burgdeeth, had never ceased to dislike her. But he was a true good man, loyal perhaps beyond all others to both Ram and Jerthon and their cause.

The fifth of those from Burgdeeth was young freckled Pol, a good-natured lad, skilled Seer, though he seldom said much. He was always there when one wanted something done, always there when a raid must be led or a scout sent out in the middle of a freezing night.

The other three Seers, two men and one woman, had lived on this land all their lives. They were good, kind folk who had used their Seer's skills to protect their land and their families and had never had the need to delve into the dark compelling skills and acquaint themselves with lurid subtleties. The two men were older, bearded and creased and very much alike, except Berd's hair and beard were white, and Erould was dark of hair and smooth-shaven. They were equally succinct and short in speech. The woman was young: a tall, square, dark-haired farmgirl who could wield sword and bow as well as any man and had a fun-loving way with the young, unmarried soldiers that added to the sharp-witted, rollicking pleasure of all concerned.

Jerthon leaned forward. They had been discussing the raids. His anger was deep, and searing. "No more than a handful of Herebian raiders—calling themselves a nation—Kubal!" His green eyes blazed.

"They would not be so free with us," Drudd countered, "were it not for BroogArl and the cursed power he has amassed!"

"It will be a touchy job setting the captives free," Jerthon said. "Even if the Kubalese prison *is* no more than a hog cage, it will be a job getting them out safe before the Kubalese shoot them from hiding, out of spite." He unrolled a mat of blank parchment and began to sketch out quick plans for defending Carriol should the need arise. Drudd made a suggestion. Pol asked about horses in the north. They had nearly agreed to all the necessary details when Jerthon saw that no one was listening, all had turned to stare beyond him to the portal. He spun around, alarmed, as the wind, risen suddenly, swept into the citadel, lifting and tearing the maps, toppling chairs as the Seers rose to crowd around the portal, staring out. And in the wild sky Horses of Eresu were battling, tossed on the wind, their great wings torn by the gale; they were swept away, they beat against the wind, forcing themselves back, powerful animals buffeted like birds as they fought toward safety. A mare was blown to the ledge, fighting to keep her balance, two stallions were tumbled, descended at last, came in beside her. The Seers moved away from the portal as six more winged ones braced against wind, then pushed inside, heads down and ears back against the onslaught. Soon the whole band had fought its way down out of the seething sky to the ledge and into the protecting grotto. The winged horses came at once to the Seers, stood close; and the Seers spoke softly to them, made their minds open and receptive; but no thought passed from one to another. As if the horses had gone mute or the Seers deaf. Jerthon stood with his hand on a brown stallion's cheek, trying to understand what had happened; what force had created such sudden chaos in the sky—though well enough he knew. Curse the Pellians! Curse this damnable silence! The dark made a web they could not penetrate. He tried to feel into the falling night for the shape and sense of the thing that had driven and buffeted the winged ones; he touched something dark and unyielding, and then his mind was torn and driven until at last he must withdraw.

A monstrous darkness lusting for blood, thriving on fear and confusion.

He sent for grains and the mild ale the winged ones so relished, and they made themselves at ease, some lying on the low stone shelves and outcroppings that had been worn smooth by their ancestors before them, some standing, still, beside the portal watching the darkening sky. When they were rested, Jerthon knew, when the danger was past, they would be off again, and the citadel would seem strangely empty.

The Seers moved among the winged horses caressing them and speaking to them with a reverence that came from awe, but too, from a gentle mutual understanding of this world that they shared so differently and yet with such like sympathies and fears. Skeelie stood beside a pale mare who seemed only slowly able to calm her terror. The winged horses had been, from her early childhood, the source of fierce wonder for Skeelie. Now, seeing them so distressed, her anger stirred painfully. Let the dark do battle with Seers, not with the gentle winged ones. Broog-Arl must hate everything beautiful, would kill all joy if he could. Surely the very essence of life, the wild freedom of the winged ones, offended him. She pressed her face against the mare's pale neck, hiding tears of helpless anger—of rage at an evil they could no longer fight, rage at a force she did not know how to battle. She thought of Ram then, suddenly, Ram moving alone toward the dark mountains, vulnerable to attack, and she went sick with apprehension. What further evil would the dark be about this night? The mare shivered. Skeelie smoothed her neck, tried to reassure her; but her terrible fear was now for Ram. She prayed silently for Ram's safety.

RAM WATCHED darkness fall. The wind swept cold and damp down from the mountains and across the hills, flattening the tall ruddy grass, blowing the horses' manes with sharp whipping motions. The darkness was early, hurried by heavy clouds. He looked toward the mountains, which were only a smear now in the falling night, and was gripped with a sudden sharp longing for the wolves, for Fawdref's wolfish grin and his cool wisdom.

It had been more than a year since they had met. Fawdref was growing old—even the great wolves grow old. Growing gray and thinner, Ram knew. He longed to go to him, to hold Fawdref's shaggy head on his shoulder, to see gentle Rhymannie bow and smile at him; to be alone inside the dark mountains and the old grottoes, among the wolves once more. But he could not.

He had reached out again and again toward Burgdeeth, trying to sense something of what was occurring there. Had Venniver another victim for his fires? But Burgdeeth remained maddeningly locked away from him. He could only hasten, now, up toward the black mountains and into them, to seek as quickly as he could the hidden valley of Eresu, and then to use every skill he possessed to gain the gods' help in stopping Venniver's insane murders.

The wind blew clouds across the stars, hiding Ere's slim moons. He could smell rain, and the wind chilled him through. He dug his leather cape from the pack none too soon, for thunder began to rattle; and then the rain itself came pelting sudden and sharp and cold. The pack mare lurched close to his knee, seeking protection. The night was black as sin, drear and damnably wet.

His leather was near soaked through and the horses drenched when he sensed suddenly that a man rode beside him, just beyond his sight in the pounding rain. He felt the rider draw closer. He could see the darker shape then, in the heavy downpour. A tall man, on a tall horse, caped, he thought, and looking down at him. He could feel his stare like a lance. Ram slipped his sword from the scabbard, more irritated than afraid, and waited. He wondered that his horses gave no sign of fear, not a twitch from his mount. He wanted badly to bark out a challenge, but held his silence.

The rider lurched suddenly so close to Ram that their boots touched, Ram's sword poised inches from his chest. And though he had to shout above the driving rain, the man's voice was uncertain and lost. "Can you tell me—I—what place is this? I seem . . . I seem to have lost my way."

Ram frowned. "You are in Carriol. We—you ride toward her western border, toward Blackcob. Where do you come from, stranger, that you are so lost as that? Where do you come from that you are out on such a night?"

"I—from the mountains. I come from the mountains and—have lost myself and could . . . I could not stay where I was. You . . ." he reached out a hand then and touched Ram's shoulder unexpectedly. Ram felt a sudden ease, a sense of comfort. "And you, lad? Unless a man were lost like me, only an urgent mission would bring him out on such a night." They were both shouting, impossible to be heard otherwise, but their words might have been spoken quietly, almost shyly.

"I ride—I ride on a private mission." Ram said warily.

"I see. And may I come along with you until I—until I get my bearings? I don't . . . Or is your mission too private to allow me that?"

"You—you may ride with me."

"There are—if we are riding toward the west hills of Carriol, there will be fences lad, in the dark . . ."

Ram frowned, puzzled. "There are few fences on this land. Though—though fences—stone walls perhaps, would be useful."

"Few fences yet? But . . ." The man went silent for a long moment, and when he spoke again it seemed to be with some care. "Carriol—Carriol is not so large a nation, then."

"Everyone in Ere, I would have thought, knows Carriol's exact size and strength."

"I have . . . I have been a long time in the mountains."

Ram's unease increased. "No man dwells for long in those mountains, stranger. No man I ever heard of."

"I come—I have traveled far into the mountains for a time—into the unknown lands these—many years. I do . . . I do not know what has happened in any of the nations of Ere. I must have been wrong about the fences, about remembering . . . You—you would favor me by telling me the news if you don't mind shouting over this damnable rain."

Ram studied the shadow that rode beside him. Who was this man? Why did he seem so confused? How could he remember fences that had never been? Ram knew he should challenge him further, question him, but he could not bring himself to do it. There was a sense of hurt about the man, as if he had suffered, as if his strange confusion came from some painful experience; he felt, suddenly, very gentle with the man, felt as if this man *needed* to know Ere's history, as if to tell him would be to help him find himself.

Ram told him, shouting through the rain, of Carriol's past from the time he had come there twelve years back, leaving out only those things that might, to the wrong ears, be harmful to Carriol. He told him something of the rising power of the dark Seers, though not all of it. The man's questions were strange, disoriented. Ram thought he was old, the timbre of his voice was of an aged man. And some of his questions seemed strange indeed, given his confusion, implied a knowledge of Ere he should not have if he had been in the mountains for years. He puzzled Ram, but did not frighten him. They rode in silence for a while, each with his own thoughts, and Ram could not touch the man's mind—though whether that was because of some skill he held, or because of the dark Seers, Ram did not know.

The heavy rain lasted full three hours across the hills to the river Urobb and did not abate as they rode up the last steep rise to the settlement of Blackcob that lay overlooking the river—though one could not see or hear the river, only driving rain. It was near midnight. Not a light shone anywhere; Blackcob was still as death and the rain likely never to end. Ram found Rolf Klingen's corral only after bruising his shins on some piled barrels and swearing a lot. The stranger followed him obediently, and it occurred to Ram as he unsaddled the gelding that he had not even asked the man's name; and perhaps he was foolish to bring him here into Blackcob, which had already seen more trouble than it wanted. Yet still he trusted the man. He unsaddled the pack mare under the shed, rubbed the horses down and, because they bumped one another in the dark, knew the stranger did the same. He felt reluctant to ask a name not given. They found grain at last and buckets; and when the animals were cared for, they went to wake old Klingen. Ram badly wanted a mug of something hot, and some food. Knowing he must have the stranger's name if they were to spend the night with Klingen, he shouted, "How are you called, stranger?" and got a mouthful of rain.

"I am Anchorstar. And you, lad?"

"Ram. You can call me Ram."

Ram felt the stranger pause in the downpour and stare, then come on again. "Ramad?" he cried, almost softly. "Ramad—Ramad of wolves, then?"

"Yes, I am Ramad. But how . . ." Cold and wet and hungry, Ram spent but little time wondering how the old man had known his name when all else about Carriol seemed so confusing to him. When the old man made no answer, he put it out of his mind and rapped sharply at Klingen's door, stood hunched under the overhang shivering, the wound in his side paining him abysmally after the long ride. What in Urdd was taking Klingen so long? He pounded again, felt Anchorstar stir beside him and push closer to the log wall. He pounded a third time, fit to break the door, then reached to lift the latch.

Chapter Four

SOME FIVE HOURS ride to the west of Blackcob it was raining equally hard. The town of Kubal showed no light, gone in sleep except for a young girl standing in the darkness of a corral, drenched with rain, weeping so violently her whole body shook with sobs; yet weeping in silence, choking back the wail of anguish that rose and twisted her, dared not be heard crying in the night or she would be beaten and the mare would be beaten again too. The mare she clung to stood hunched and strangely twisted, a big mare, Telien had to reach to caress her warm, wet neck, caress carefully so as not to touch the bloody wounds. She had staunched some of the blood, though it was impossible to bandage the whip-cuts across the mare's back and legs, impossible to bandage, without further hurting, her poor maimed wings: wings once marvels of light-flung beauty, now clipped to the skin like a barn fowl's, naked and bony and deformed-looking, with a few ragged feathers clinging, and bloody where AgWurt had cut too close. Telien could not erase the picture of the mare lying tangled in AgWurt's snare, there in the valley, bound down with ropes; the picture of AgWurt's face as he lashed her again and again so Telien turned away, sick, "My own father! I would . . . I would kill him if I could!" Though she knew, ashamed, that she was too terrified of him to try.

Chapter Four

The mare reached around to nuzzle her in loving warmth. Telien hugged her gently, stood drenched by rain and felt only the mare's warmth and her own sickness at what AgWurt had done.

There was no roof to shelter the mare, and Telien could not get her out of the corral for it was locked and AgWurt carried his keys, always, chained securely to his wrist. She could not bring herself to leave the mare alone in the dark and rain, had been here since AgWurt went to bed. She began to talk to the mare, for perhaps the sound of her voice would help somehow. She thought that a wild creature, injured so, would only want to die. She must give the mare what love she could, what hope. She began to speak, very softly, putting all the love she had into the words; though the words she used meant little for they could not understand one another. Only one who was Seer-born could speak with the winged ones.

"I used to come to watch you. No one knew I did. I came at night, or when they were all away raiding. I found the secret valley. You—you were the most beautiful of all, like—like a golden shaft of sun leaping in the sky and then falling to earth, then sweeping up again. I used to watch you drifting on the winds and then grazing in the deep grass and your wings spreading out just with the pure joy of *being!* Oh, it was lovely. You were lovely, you were like . . . You will be free again," she said, her voice trembling. "Your wings will grow whole again, I promise you. The muscles are not cut, he would not *injure* your wings, he wants . . ." She pressed her face against the mare. "I didn't *know.* I never knew that AgWurt followed me!" The mare nuzzled her softly. "I would have died before I let AgWurt know!" The mare moved her nose, shifted her weight as if the pain had increased. "Maybe he followed me when—the night the darkness came over the valley. You saw it, all of you saw that darkness. You flew away at once. Was AgWurt behind me then, was that the noise I heard and thought it was part of—of the cold dark thing in the sky? What *was* that dark? Like a great monster only—only all cloudy and boiling along the top of the hills. So fast! So silent and black. The feel of it! Oh, it was *evil!*" She shivered, remembering. "But then AgWurt must have come back later to set the snares." She shuddered. "I'm glad the others got away, but you . . ." she glanced at the mare's swollen belly. "You could not. Your colt—I wanted—I wanted to kill AgWurt. I wanted to cut you free but . . ." Shame engulfed Telien again. "I wasn't brave enough. I thought he would kill me instead, and that he would kill you too." Her voice shook. "I couldn't watch him beat you, I turned my face away."

For some time she was silent. She wished she had the power of Seeing so they could speak with one another. Sometimes, lying in the brush at the edge of the hidden valley, she had known just from their actions what the winged horses must be saying to one another with their silent, loving ways.

AgWurt meant to break the mare's will. He meant to subdue her until she was as nothing, make of her a tame, domestic animal submissive to him. He meant to do the same to her colt, to clip its wings and make it slave to him. He did not dream that that was impossible—to AgWurt nothing was impossible if he put enough force to it. Telien knew the mare would die first, before she would be slave; that she would likely kill her colt rather than let AgWurt lay hands on it. AgWurt envisioned himself mounted on a winged horse of Eresu; he thought he would be like Ramad of the wolves then, like Jerthon of Carriol. An invincible warrior. AgWurt's dreams sickened her. "I saw you with your stallion," Telien said softly. "He is—he is like fire! Like flame in the sky!" To think of a winged colt born to the captivity of AgWurt's heart-breaking treatment, earthbound and fenced, was unbearable. "I will get you away from him somehow—*somehow* I will!

The mare shifted then and turned to look straight at her, lifting her head in pride, and Telien knew suddenly and with terrible joy that the mare did, indeed, understand her. She didn't know how, without Seer's skill to link them. She didn't care how. The wonder of it made her tremble. She said softly, "Meheegan, Meheegan," for the mare had given her her name. The sudden illuminating knowledge of the mare's name was like honey, like a song within Telien. "You will be free, Meheegan. I promise you will." And she knew she would kill AgWurt if she must and hoped she would be brave enough.

RAM POUNDED AGAIN, swearing. Klingen must sleep like a stone. He was chilled through, his temper gone, his wound painful from the long ride, his bandage soaked with rain or blood or both. Beside him Anchorstar was silent, lost in incredible patience. At last Ram lifted the latch and kicked Klingen's door open, stepping back in case someone else was there. He had no taste for battling some errant band of Herebians in the middle of this cursed wet night.

No candle flared. No voice rang out. He edged in at last, cautiously, felt Anchorstar behind him, found flint and a small taper under his leather cape and struck light.

But the light showed nothing. There were no walls. He was not inside the cabin though the doorframe pressed hard and real against his arm. Anchorstar touched his shoulder, Ram felt the man's fear. They faced, not the homely cabin room but a void: inside the door vast space yawned, swallowing Ram's light so the taper's glow was only a useless pool lost at once in the yawning emptiness. They had come through Klingen's door, where Ram had come a hundred times—Ram knew a cot should stand just there, a cookfire there with a pot at the back—but he stood instead on the brink of empty blackness and felt Anchorstar draw his breath in fear. Incredible space loomed inside that door, space empty filled with a monstrous cold as if the world ended at their feet.

A voice whispered out, barely discernible yet echoing, a cold voice calling to Ram from no direction and from all directions, and it did not speak in words but soothed him and enticed him; the emptiness soothed and reached around him, holding him as a woman would, so his pain and hunger were gone and he was warm and incredibly comforted. He forgot Anchorstar. He just had to step forward, be soothed—he froze suddenly with the sense of BroogArl all around him, the sense of HarThass himself risen from death to haunt him with the bones of living skeletons from his childhood agonies. Drawn forward against his will, he clung to the doorframe sick and shaken as BroogArl reached, enticed—BroogArl would fling him into the endless dark, and Ram could not resist. . . . He felt Anchorstar grip his shoulder suddenly, and he was spun away from the door, jerked back into the rain, stumbled terrified into the welcome drenching.

He stood shaken and weak, clinging to Anchorstar, and felt hands on his shoulders then guiding him into the hut where a welcome fire blazed.

Anchorstar pushed him into a chair, and old Klingen held his arm as though he might fall. The kettle was boiling, the hut warm and homey. Klingen stared at him puzzled, his brown seamed face and brown hair hardly distinguishable from the rough wood walls of the hut, as if part of the hut itself had come alive to produce the old man, brown wrinkled skin, brown rough nightshirt like bark, even his voice creaking like too-dry wood.

"Iee, Ram, you give me a scare! What was you two

doing standing there staring in at me like you'd seen a living ghost and me having to ask you five times to come in before you ever so much as heard me! Come, off with those clothes, both of you, and get youselves up to the fire." Klingen turned and began to stir up a pot hanging at the side of the fire, then reached an earthen jug from the shelf and poured out generous lacings into mugs, poured in hot water from the kettle. "Here, you two, this'll take the chill off'n ya."

Ram drank the hot liquor so greedily it burned all the way down.

"There, lad, take off the bandages too—I'll rout out some clean rags." Then, staring as Ram undid the bandages, "Sure you took one right in the liver near, didn't you." Ram was relieved to see that all the wetness was no more than rain, that no blood oozed. Anchorstar sat quietly at the table wrapped in something shapeless of Klingen's, watching them both with a puzzled look; a tall thin man he was, with hair white as loess dust and eyes—Ram stared. He had never seen yellow eyes in a man. In a goat, perhaps, in a wild creature. The wolves had yellow eyes. But never yellow eyes in a man, eyes completely strange under that shock of white hair. And in spite of his quiet repose, he seemed ill at ease in a way, as if this world of log hut and friendly fire were almost foreign to him.

As Klingen stirred the pot, a fine aroma filled the hut, and soon enough the old man set bowls of steaming stew before them rich with gravy, and new bread, and refilled their mugs with the strong honeyrot and hot water, very little of the latter so that soon a fine maze filled Ram's mind and, with full stomach, he wanted only sleep. But the two older men had set to talking, and Ram could not close his eyes for the strangeness of the conversation as Klingen tried to winnow out Anchorstar's identity as a mouse would winnow out grain from sealed stores. Where had Anchorstar come from, and why? Anchorstar, at first reluctant, began at last to speak of the far mountains and of lands where none of Ere had ever ventured, to speak of the old mythical animals that still existed there, of the triebuck and the great dragoncats; and of the gantroed, which Ram knew well from the time on Tala-charen. He spoke of wonders Ram had only dreamed, but he did not speak of *when* he had gone into the far lands, of how many years ago, or from whence he came. When he rose at last to open his pack, he took from it a small leather pouch and spilled out across the table a cluster of shimmering jewels. Ram and Klingen stared. Never had Ram seen such stones, deep amber, filled with light. Ram held one before the fire and its colors flashed as if it had absorbed the fire, and from its center a gleaming star shone out.

"How are they called?" Klingen asked, drawing in his breath.

"They are starfires; they are said to bring luck, though I cannot vouch for that. They are said by some to bring . . ." He paused, stared at Ram with that deep, yellow-eyed look that Ram could not plumb. "They are said to give to man a lightness of spirit, a lightness of being that will—that can do magical things. Though not," he added, "not like the runestone of Eresu."

"You know of the runestone?"

"Many in Ere knew of the runestone long before I—before I touched the unknown lands. I know of Tala-charen and of the splitting of the stone." Anchorstar leaned back and touched his empty bowl lightly, then pushed it aside. "I know that Ramad of—Ramad of wolves is . . ." He paused for a long moment, studying Ram, "is of great importance to Ere, to what—to what will happen in Ere."

Ram searched his face, could not discern his exact meaning. Whether of hidden sarcasm—though he thought not—or of prophesy; or of something else far more certain. Anchorstar's steady eyes seemed very certain.

"With the whole runestone," Ram said, "perhaps I might be of importance to Ere. Perhaps. But the runestone is destroyed. Only a shard remains."

A shift in the light of Anchorstar's eyes might have been only the dance of firelight. "You are—one dedicated to the good, Ramad of wolves. Whatever comes to your hand will be used to the good of Ere. And if the runestone—the whole stone . . ." But he did not finish, turned away almost as if in sorrow, and sat gazing into Klingen's fire.

At last Ram stirred and spoke. "And you, Anchorstar. What are you dedicated to?" For this tall white-haired man, whose look Ram could not fathom, was more than a traveler, more than a wanderer upon Ere. There was a dedication in him, a purpose in him strong as steel.

Anchorstar turned back to look at him. "A trader, Ramad. I am a trader." He held up one of the amber stones. "What I traded for these stones was little. What I will trade them for could—could be much."

In the cold dawn, with the rain abated but the sky dull gray, Blackcob looked forlorn indeed. The Kubalese attack had left burned huts and sheds, burned fences, grain stores scattered uselessly where the side of a shed had been broken away, very few horses in the corrals, and they the dregs of the lot. Ram found Anchorstar out well before him tending to his mount, and that mount made Ram stare with wonder. He had had no glimpse of him last night as they rubbed down and fed their horses in darkness. A tall, beautifully made stallion, dun in color, as steel gray as the morning sky.

Never had there been such a horse in Ere, such a magnificent, long-legged, short-coupled stallion; he was exactly what Ram and Jerthon had dreamed of, the fine wide eyes, the strong light bones—he could have been a product of their own breeding program many years hence. This dun stallion was not of Ere, never. Had Anchorstar found him somewhere beyond the far mountains; were there men there to breed such as this?

And when he questioned Anchorstar, Anchorstar's confusion made him press his querying obstinately. Did the horse come from Moramia or Karra, or from somewhere on the high desert where the secretive tribes dwelt? Anchorstar would not say. Did he come from the far lands? Were there men there so skilled at the breeding of horses?

"He comes," Anchorstar said at last, "from very far. Farther than you imagine." Again there was the sadness, like a darkened cloak swirling around Anchorstar. "Yet this stallion is closer to you, Ramad, than you know."

"And will you sell him to me, then? He would be the finest blood in our breeding, he . . ."

"I know, Ramad of wolves, what he would do. But I cannot sell him. I cannot part with him in—I cannot part with him now." Anchorstar would say no more, Ram could not get him to speak further of the stallion and gave it up at last.

They rode out of Blackcob together after Klingen's huge breakfast, Anchorstar huddled in his cape but sitting his mount lightly, hardly needing to touch the reins.

Ram's wound, freshly bound, did not pain him now. He had slept dreamless and deep, warmed by Klingen's fire without and by Klingen's numerous cups of hot honeyrot within, lulled by old Klingen's snoring like wild hogs rattling—Anchorstar had snored not at all. Ram did not lead the pack mare now, had left her for the men of Blackcob. They would need every mount they could get to make the ride into Kubal two days hence.

He parted from Anchorstar at the forking of the rivers

Urobb and Voda Cul. Ram headed up the eastern shore of the Urobb toward the dark mountains, on toward the valley of the gods, keeping well away from Kubalese eyes. Anchorstar rode direct for Kubal, against both Ram's and Klingen's advice.

"They will kill you for the stallion, if nothing else. And those stones; if the Kubalese see the starfires . . ."

"I must take my chances. I would—I would see this Kubal that has risen on the hills."

He would say no more. Ram stared after him, puzzling. He rode at a gallop toward the low, western hills, his white hair like a flag on the morning.

Surely he did not travel to Kubal merely from curiosity. Klingen had described the Kubalese raids adequately, described their brutality with sufficient clarity to belay any idle curiosity a man might have.

Ram forded the Voda Cul at the shallows, then veered north of the Urobb, farther from Kubal's prying eyes. He took his noon meal from the saddle while his gelding drank, and soon was among high foothills and narrow valleys where the rich grass was crossed by small wandering springs. The dark humping mountains rose directly over him, gigantic peaks laid about by deep shadow and blackened by falls of volcanic stone, empty wild mountains peopled only by the wolves and, here and there, by the winged horses transient as moths on the wind. There were caves in the mountains, immense and twilit and filled with the wonders of a time long past. Ram thought of the caves he knew, and longed for the warmth of shaggy muzzles thrust deep into his hands, for the rank musty smell and the deep voices of the wolves, for Fawdref's knowing grin. He slipped the wolf bell from inside his tunic and held it for a long painful time, staring at the rearing bitch wolf holding the bell in her mouth, remembering. Remembering so much. Fear, terror. Such warmth, opening his mind to wonders he had not dreamed. The sense of brotherhood, greeting the great wolves and knowing, always, that he had come home. He longed to go to them. But he could not pause nor turn aside, he must go quickly into Eresu lest, while he tarried, another child should burn at Venniver's abominable sacrifice. He pushed the bay gelding restlessly toward the dark peaks where lay the hidden valley. Soon he would stand facing the gods, their bodies glinting and ever changing as if they moved in another element. He went weak with awe and with apprehension. *Could* a man approach the gods? His appalling effrontery at considering he could do so, could solicit the gods' help, nearly undid him.

Yet it must be done. Nothing else short of war—and Carriol was not strong enough now, crippled by the dark, to make such war—could prevent Venniver's slaughter of the Seeing children. Could prevent Venniver's insane and false religion from creating untold destruction and pain.

And if he had ever thought, as a child, that the gods were not truly gods, were, as he had once told Tayba, only different from men, he trembled now at that thought.

Soon he entered a valley that rose steeply toward a grove of young trees thrusting up between stones of black lava. Beyond the trees rose steep grassy banks. He saw the winged horses suddenly, for they were standing in shadow by the grove, motionless, watching him approach, five winged ones, their dark eyes knowing, their wings folded tight to their bodies to avoid the low branches of the wood. They seemed—they were waiting for him, yet their thoughts did not touch him. His horse stared uncertainly, smelled them, saw their wings, and wanted to bolt. A big russet stallion came forward lifting his wings, touched Ram's cheek with his muzzle, ignored Ram's mount utterly. He pushed at Ram's red hair with his nose, a gesture of respect and love. They had some need, these winged ones, some trouble. Ram tried to understand and could not, the dark held impenetrable silence over them, silence between those who should speak with one another as easily as breathing. At last, unable to communicate, the stallion led Ram deep into the wood. The four other winged ones followed.

There, just in the dappled shade, a winged colt stood twisted into ungainly position, caught in a rope snare. Ram dismounted, drew his knife. The colt was big, a yearling, and had been cut cruelly by the ropes as he fought to free himself. Ram could see where the stout lines had been chewed by the other horses. He began to cut the snare away.

He had cut nearly all the ropes when suddenly his arm touched a rope yet uncut, saplings hissed and a second snare sprang, jerking and choking him as he fought, engulfing him in tangles. And he heard a human shout and suddenly five riders came plunging down the hill. He fought in desperation, slashed at ropes. The winged ones turned, screaming, to battle the riders. Ram, fearing more for them than for himself, shouted them away, saw the colt leap skyward, then the others, as bows were drawn against them with steel-tipped arrows, heard a mare scream as she took an arrow in the leg. The five horses lifted fast into the wind.

The riders circled Ram. A dark Herebian warrior swung down from the saddle, his leather vest marked with the black cross of Kubal, his brutal face close to Ram's as Ram struggled in fury against the ropes. He was a head taller than Ram and stank of sweat. He jerked Ram up, signaled that Ram's horse be brought, did not speak, seemed furious that the colt had escaped. But he was sharply interested in Ram, kept staring at his red hair and grinning. The other two men jumped at his bidding like puppets on a stick.

They brought Ram's horse. Ram fought them uselessly, was too tightly bound to do little more than give them a bruise or two as they tied his hands and feet, then removed the snare and threw him over his saddle, tied him down like a sack of meal so tight the wolf bell pressed sharply into his ribs and the saddle tore at his healing wound. The men reset the snare, then led Ram's horse lurching up the hill.

Ram's wound burned like fire. Surely it was torn open. He thought he could feel blood running. Evening fell, the night deepened. Every bone in his body ached from riding belly down across the saddle. The journey seemed to go on forever. It was very late indeed when his horse was led at last into the Kubalese camp.

Chapter Five

Lights swung wildly in Ram's face, voices shouted, more lights were flung up so men could stare at him. His horse shied and spun. He wanted to kill every man in the compound, but was helpless as a babe. Numb and cold, likely all his ribs broken after that abominable ride, and the wolf bell had gouged a raw place and his wound was one screaming pain. If he could get his hands on just one . . .

A lantern was shoved into his face, blinding him. When his vision cleared at last, he could see corral fences in the swinging lights, and some sheds. Men crowded around him. Someone poked his wound bringing pain like a knife. Someone jerked his plunging horse until it stilled.

"Fires of Urdd, a Seer! AgWurt has brung us a Seer!" A hank of Ram's hair was pulled, bringing a roar of laughter.

"A better day's work than one o' them unnatural winged horses, I say!"

"Where'd they get a Seer?"

"Look, 'E's a young one, looks—them's Carriol clothes, this . . ."

"It's the wolf one, Brage! They call Ramad! Ramad of wolves, this! Why . . ."

"They'll pay a price for this one in Carriol! Better than a flying horse, AgWurt! Better . . ."

Ram was poked and exclaimed over, then at last was left to himself still tied face down across the saddle, much later was cut loose and jerked roughly off his horse to drop in the mud, so stiff he could hardly roll away from the gelding's hooves. Someone jerked him up, and he was dragged, still bound, to a pen of thick crossed bars, was shoved inside with such force he fell against a post and lay with his head reeling.

No one bothered to untie him. The mud in which he lay was redolent with manure. He was too weary to try to rise. He heard a lock snap shut. He must have slept in spite of pain, for when he was aware of anything again the night was still and much colder and there were no lights, just the thin glow of the two moons that had risen higher and were reflected in puddles in the mud. What had waked him? His hands and feet were numb from the bindings, and icy cold. Someone whispered close beside him, a girl's voice.

She was reaching through the bars, holding out a mug. "Try to move your hands, I've taken off the ropes. Try—can you move your feet?"

He reached out, could hardly feel the mug, had to consciously direct his fingers to close around it; drank greedily.

"You are in Kubal," she whispered. "My father caught you in a snare meant for . . ."

"For the horses of Eresu." Ram's voice was hoarse.

"Yes. I tried—I can't reach your bandage. It's bloody. Is the pain very great?"

"I'm all right." He touched numb fingers to his side, felt the wetness; then pulled himself up until he could lean against the wooden cage. She drew back, startled, seemed suddenly uneasy at his closeness. He caught the smooth, slim turn of her cheek, a brief glimpse in the thin wash of moonlight, then she was in shadow again;

a strange, stirring glimpse that unsettled him for no reason.

She had lifted her hand, now she touched the fence, seemed lost in some depth of thought he had no way to follow. She said at last, urgently, "Why were you there in the foothills? Did you mean to come to Kubal, Seer?"

"I—I am of Carriol." She was watching him so intently, almost as if he frightened her. Why was she here in the dark by his pen, why was she helping him? "I was traveling away from Kubal, I was traveling toward the mountains."

She moved until she could see his face more clearly in the faint moonlight. He was covered with mud and dung, a pretty sight. She almost reached again, drew her hand back. "You are . . . you are Ramad."

"How did they know me, those men?"

"There are fifteen Seers in Carriol. Jerthon of Carriol is older than you. There are some old men, some women. There is only one other young man, and he is thin and freckled, older. There is only one as young as you and red of hair. And brazen sometimes, so the captives say."

He grinned. "Tell me your name."

"I am Telien."

"Yes, Telien. You freed a woman and her daughters and they came to us." He wanted to tell her something, to share with her something, but he did not know what. He wanted to give her something. "I was riding toward Eresu," he blurted, and he had not meant to tell anyone this. He saw her eyes widen: green eyes, cool green in the glancing moonlight. He wanted to touch her cheek and didn't understand his feelings. She studied his face, and he was stirred by her, and restless and afraid. What was this strangeness? He felt a closeness to her like nothing he could remember, a closeness as brothers of blood would feel, yet not like that at all; the closeness of a woman, but unlike what he had felt for any woman.

How could a man feel tenderness, feel passion, kneeling in the muck of a corral, freezing cold? Yet he felt all this for Telien. She started to speak but a lantern flared nearby, and at once she was gone into the night as if she had never been.

When he woke again it was dawn, and some chidrack were screaming and pecking after bugs at one side of his pen. He rolled over, stared at the crossed bars. He had been sleeping in the mud like an animal. He rose painfully, saw the ropes lying half buried in the mud, and remembered Telien. He moved stiffly, every bone ached, and his wound pulled painfully. His stomach was empty as a cavern, his mouth dry. Hardly light, nothing stirred. There were no cobbled streets here, only mud. No stone houses. Rough wooden sheds, many pens. No smoke from the tin chimneys yet. He stood looking through the bars, knowing he should try to make a plan of escape and unable to think of anything but Telien.

At last he stirred himself, found the gate to his pen, and began to examine the lock, a huge heavy thing set into wide steel straps so it could not be pried loose. He gave it up finally and turned once more to sorting out his surroundings.

The nearby pens held horses slogging in mud so it was a wonder they weren't all lame. In a far corral human captives slept on the ground like dead bodies—could have been bodies scattered, except some of them snored. In a corral to his left stood a great mare, her rump turned to him. She—he stared, not believing what he saw. When she turned, he caught his breath.

A mare of Eresu! And her wings shorn bare so he went sick at the sight of her. Wings clipped to the skin like some fettered barn fowl, wings made ugly and monstrous, misshapen, held tight to her sides in pain or in shame, ungainly bony protuberances that once had been graceful arcs commanding winds, commanding the skies of Ere. Her body was covered with the long welts of a lash, cruel and deep.

He tried to reach her with his thoughts, but she stood hunched and unresponding. How long had she been in this place? Had she been captured in AgWurt's snares? What did AgWurt intend for her? To clip her wings like this, to cripple her—and the poor mare was heavy with foal. What did he want? Only to bedevil and degrade these wild creatures whose spirits he could not touch? Or to ride them, to become their masters in some sick-minded attempt at mastering that which no man could ever master.

He turned his attention again to the compound. He could not help the mare, not yet. But AgWurt shared now in the cold, purposeful hatred Ram held for Venniver who burned children, and for the dark Pellian Seers.

The sky was growing lighter, the compound taking fuller shape. There was a long shed beyond the pens that could be a central kitchen and sleeping hall, perhaps an arms store as well. How many men did the encampment house? He could see another row of sheds some distance beyond the first, and more corrals. He counted sixty-two horses, some of them very good mounts, many from Carriol. He caught his breath when he saw the dun stallion standing tall among the other mounts.

And where was Anchorstar, then? He could not see him among the prisoners. He stood looking, outraged, uncertain. Was the tall, white-haired man sleeping in the hall among the Kubalese? Was he friend to the Kubalese, had he spoken to Ram in deceit?

Had he alerted the Kubalese that Ram was near, traveling alone?

He could hardly believe that, and yet . . . why had Anchorstar come here? What business could the man have with the Kubalese?

In the closest prison pen, figures were beginning to rise stiffly from the mud where they had slept. Ram watched them, hoping to see Anchorstar among them, but assuming he would not; and Anchorstar was not among them. When Ram turned, Telien stood beside his cage.

Her green eyes, the shock of recognition he felt for her held him frozen. Her face so familiar, he knew it so well; yet he had hardly seen her before this moment, seen only her moon-touched shadow last night. But he *had* seen her, knew well the tone of her skin, the curve of her cheek just there—and suddenly without warning he knew, went weak with knowing: Time spun, twelve years disappeared, and he was caught again in the vortex of Time spinning at the top of Tala-charen. Telien was there among the shadowy figures; thunder rumbled and the mountain shook; he saw her pale hair fall across her shoulders as it now fell, her green eyes watching him as they now watched; saw the jade shard in her hands turning slowly from white hot to deep green; and she disappeared.

And Telien stood holding out a plate of bread and meat, puzzled by his scowl, uncomprehending. He took the plate woodenly. She frowned, trying to understand, did not speak. He gripped her wrist so she stared back at him in alarm, then with pain; but she showed no sign of the recognition he felt.

He could not gather words. When he released her, she continued to stare, unable to turn away.

He swallowed, found his voice at last, stared at her pale hair, her golden skin, seeing her still as she was in Tala-charen—exactly as she was now. "Do you not remember, Telien?" How could she not remember? She had been there. "You held the runestone in your hands—the runestone of Eresu."

"The runestone of Eresu?" She frowned, studying his face. "You make fun of me, Ramad of wolves. The runestone of Eresu lies in the sacred tower of Carriol. How could I have held it?"

"You did not hold that stone, Telien. You held its mate. You held it and you . . ." He stopped speaking, could not explain, was gripped with such longing for her; and with a sudden longing for Tala-charen and for that moment that had caused him such pain. She touched his cheek hesitantly; they saw a figure emerge from the hall and she left him at once slipping away, did not return until night.

He gazed after her, trying to understand. Why did she not remember?

She had brought bandages, salve. At last he busied himself with changing the dressing of his wound. He did not like the look of it, angry and swollen, torn open where it had earlier begun to heal; very painful. He was leaning tiredly against the wooden bars feeling light-headed when he saw, so suddenly he jerked upright, the tall, lean figure of Anchorstar going across the compound led by two soldiers, the old man's hair white as snow in the dull morning. Ram nearly cried out, held his tongue with effort, watched as the soldiers pushed Anchorstar roughly into the long hall and pulled the door closed behind them.

They had come from the direction of the prison pens. Surely Anchorstar was captive, then, and not a friend of the Kubalese as Ram had feared. He had thought of Anchorstar as friend, had trusted him even with so short a meeting, felt for the old man a kinship it was difficult to explain. He remembered, now, Anchorstar's words as they sat before Klingen's fire. *You are one dedicated to the good, Ramad of wolves. Whatever comes to your hand will be used to the good of Ere.* No pronouncement at all of his own position, yet Ram had felt with every fiber of his Seer's strength that Anchorstar was as committed as he to the good of Carriol, of Ere.

But was feeling, even a Seer's feeling, ever enough?

He stood pondering this when the vision came, abruptly: Anchorstar kneeling before AgWurt, held like a dog, beaten by guards so the lashes cut through his leather jerkin and into his skin. Anchorstar, silent and ungiving; Anchorstar beaten raw and still unwilling to speak. What did they want of him? Ram gripped the bars, Seeing with terrible clarity. Saw, then, the small leather pouch in AgWurt's fist, knew he had taken it from Anchorstar's tunic, the starfire pouch, heard AgWurt's words briefly before the vision faded: *you* will *tell me where! I will know where they came from, or you will die in Kubal's pens, old man!*

When Telien returned, she came from the direction of the mare's fence. He had not seen her go there in the dark; her hands were freezing, as if she had been standing a long time inside that corral. The night was broken by loud voices and laughter from the hall, as if AgWurt's men sat drinking there. A thin fog lay across the moons. He wanted to look into Telien's face, but she stood with her back to the dull moonlight. She had brought meat and bread. He reached through the bars, touched her hand. She pushed the plate at him, seemed shy and confused. When she looked at him, it was with veiled, wary eyes; and yet he thought there was more. Something . . .

She said, abruptly, without greeting, "He keeps—AgWurt keeps the key chained to his wrist." As if she had thought all day about how to set him free. "I—he almost never takes it off. Once, by the water trough . . ."

"Yes, when you freed Mawn Paula and her children."

"Yes." She moved along the fence until Ram had turned so the faint moonlight fell on his face. She reached as if she would touch his hair, then stilled her hand, remained silent, watching him.

He wanted to whisper to her, to hold her.

"You can't *dig* out, Ram. The posts are buried a long way and the ground is like rock."

He touched her hand, her cheek—that face he had seen in dreams for half his life. Why didn't she remember? He wanted to speak of Tala-charen and could not.

"I can steal a knife, though. If you . . ."

He searched her eyes. So direct, so concerned for him. "A knife, yes. If I could get AgWurt to enter this cursed pen . . ." Should he speak of this? AgWurt was, after all, her father.

"If you could do that, you could kill him and take the key. I want to kill him. I am—I am afraid. I have tried. He—he wakes in his sleep. It is the—the only way I know to do it, in his sleep, and I can't even do that."

"He will die," Ram promised. "He needs to die. Is this . . . Telien, is this why you help me? Only so I will kill AgWurt?"

She looked shocked, drew back. "I—I suppose it is, in part. But . . ." She came close again. "But there is more to it than that, Ramad. I don't understand. I would help you anyway, you are a Seer of Carriol. But . . ." She was so close to him. "There is something more that I do not understand." She searched his face, trying to make sense of it. "We are together. In a way I do not understand." Was there a glint of fear on her cheek? He seemed unable to tell her how he felt. They stood on the brink of wonder beyond any he had ever known, and he could not speak. The moment on Tala-charen was a part of it, he could almost feel again Time warping, space warping beyond comprehension to form new patterns—and then suddenly terror gripped him. Terror for Telien swept him as he Saw her sucked through the barrier of time in a vision so abrupt, so lucid, a vision of Telien's fate . . . Gone. Lost in Time, perhaps for eternity.

It could not be! He would not let it be! He felt her stir

and found he was gripping her hard, hurting her. He loosed her. She touched his clenched fist. For an instant she thought his pain was from the wound and then, watching him, she knew it was not; she saw his fear and her eyes were huge with it.

When he did not move or speak, did not draw himself from the vision that held him, she dug anxious fingers into his arm and reached to turn his face to her. "*What* is *it, Seer? What vision holds you?*"

His fear for her and his sudden rending pain for himself because of it, his pain for the two of them, shook him utterly. He could not touch the edges of the vision, nor grasp the causes of the chasm of time through which he saw her fall. He could only taste his own fear and then his terrible, unbearable aloneness.

She watched him with sudden growing understanding—at least of what he felt, of what she herself felt. Of what she had felt last night, this strangeness, this sense of having known him always. She was amazed and shaken by it. There had been men; this was not like that. This was as if a part of her had suddenly, irrevocably, come home. As if her very soul had come to her suddenly out of unimaginable space.

She bent forward so her cheek was pressed against the bars and drew him to her. He held her fiercely in a grip he could not quell, kissed her, was unaware of the bars pressing into his side and shoulder; they clung together wounded by the bars of his cage, clung with a terrible sudden knowledge; and a sudden awesome fear that would, never again, quite fade.

For long after Telien left him, he paced, could not settle to sleep. Long after the warriors' voices died and lanterns were extinguished so the compound lay dark, he walked the perimeter of his pen, examining again and again his feelings for Telien.

Had they always been linked in some crevice of fate that had swept them incredibly to this place at this time? Had they always been one by some turn of their very spirits that neither one understood?

And why, then, did Telien not remember?

He woke. Something was screaming, he thought it was a woman, then knew it was not: Terrifying animal screams, nearly human, a scream more of rage than of pain. He flung up, trying to locate the direction while still half-asleep. The night was clear, the stars uncovered, the moons brighter. There was wild stirring in the winged mare's corral. She screamed again, Ram saw her rear up, saw the broad figure of a man pulling at her rope. She reared again as he spun in a dance around her trying to throw a saddle on her back. Ram could smell honeyrot, watched AgWurt's clumsy movements with fury. The man was dead drunk, meant to saddle a mare of Eresu and ride her. Ram tore at his bars uselessly, calling Agwurt every filth he could name, but the Herebian leader paid no attention. He had the mare snubbed now against the fence, had the saddle on in spite of her fighting, and was reaching to pull the girth under her belly when she kicked him so hard she sent him sprawling in the mud. But he was up again, animallike in his rage. He set on her, beating her with the bridle. Ram tried with all his skill to weaken the man, tried and could do nothing, was sweating with effort, calling the powers of the wolf bell, could not touch AgWurt. The man had succeeded in getting the saddle girthed as the mare fought uselessly against the tight snub. He was trying to mount her and so drunk he fell twice. She struck at him, screaming. Ram could sense soldiers in the darkness watching, routed from sleep, sniggering. The mare's poor wings flailed uselessly, pitifully.

Ram felt the wind, heard the rush of wings, looked

up to see the stars blotted away as dark wings swept overhead, heard the stallion's screams challenge AgWurt, saw the great horse descend in rushing flight.

The stallion dropped straight for her pen like a hunting falcon, then startled suddenly, leaped skyward again, great wings pulling as he sensed the pen too small and that he would be trapped there, his wings entangled. He hovered in confusion, wanting to get at AgWurt, then dropped down outside her pen striking at the fence in a frenzy, thrusting himself against the rails, his need to free her terrible, his need to kill AgWurt terrible. He would tear himself to pieces. Lights flared as running men struck flints, lamps caught. The great horse spun to face the shouting soldiers, pawed as they surrounded him. The soldiers fell back, their lanterns swinging wild arcs. Ram saw AgWurt slip out of the mare's pen, stealthy, rope held low, could feel AgWurt's lust as he leaped for the stallion's head.

He tried for the stallion's head and the stallion struck him, he was down under the horse's hooves, rolled free beneath the fence as the stallion lunged at him screaming with fury. Ram gasped as AgWurt drew his steel blade and came out under the bars crouched, stalking the winged horse of Eresu, meaning to kill; and then Telien was there snatching away a soldier's lantern, facing AgWurt. The man swung around, his raised blade close to her, and she flung the lantern, splashing oil across him. Fire caught at once. AgWurt screamed, aflame. Soldiers threw him to the ground, stifling flame with their own bodies.

AgWurt rose at last, limping, white with fury. He advanced on Telien coldly, slowly. She stood her ground, staring at him, Ram could not tell whether in rage or in terror. Ram's hands were bleeding from fighting the walls of his pen. AgWurt would kill her. He clutched the wolf bell in a desperate bid for power; but the dark Seers held him immobile, emasculated of all Seer's power. It was then the winged stallion spun, struck AgWurt full in the face, struck again, felling AgWurt, towered over his fallen body pounding with hooves like steel, tearing him, screaming, his rage like the sky breaking open.

The soldiers had fallen back. One raised a bow. The stallion spun again and sent him sprawling. Several men dropped their swords and ran. AgWurt lay crushed beneath the stallion's hooves, and the great horse loomed over him still, challenging soldiers; and then the stallion reared over Telien, and the soldier who held her loosed her and fled.

Now the stallion stood quietly beside Telien. She leaned for a moment against his shoulder, trembling. Then she turned to where her father lay.

AgWurt's arm was bent beneath him, his body bloody and crushed. Telien knelt, her face twisted. Would she weep for her father now? Ram watched her steadily.

Slowly she turned AgWurt's bloody body and pulled his arm from beneath him. She glanced up at Ram, removed the iron bracelet from the bleeding wrist, and let Agwurt's hand drop.

She saw the lump under his tunic then, paused, then drew out the small leather pouch and pulled it open, spilling starfires into her palm, catching her breath. She looked up at Ram, this time with wonder, tipped the starfires back into the bag, and dropped the bag into her pocket. Then she rose without another glance at AgWurt.

She unlocked Ram's pen first, then the mare's. When she had removed the saddle, the mare nudged her gently, then broke away at once in a lame gallop up through the camp and out toward the dark mountains. The stallion remained facing the soldiers with flaring nostrils, his ears flat to his head. No man dared move before him. As Ram and Telien started toward the pens of the captives, one soldier tried to draw bow, and the stallion struck him down. He did not move again.

They released the prisoners. Men flocked to catch and saddle horses, to pack the food stores, to take up weapons. Telien found herbs and bandages for those who must be tended. Children too small to ride by themselves would ride before their elders; the sick and the injured would have the one wagon. A dozen men guarded AgWurt's soldiers. The stallion had gone now, leaping into the sky to follow his mare and guard her, she who went helplessly earthbound through the night mountains heavy with foal and unable to fly to safety; for though the great wolves were her friends, the common wolves of the mountains were not, the common wolves would take pleasure in her flesh.

When Ram turned to looking for Anchorstar, he was gone. No one had seen him. The dun stallion was gone, Anchorstar's saddle, every sign of him. Telien could not remember when she had last seen that white head among the prisoners, seen the dun stallion. When she reached into her pocket to draw out the little pouch of starfires, it too was gone; one stone gleamed with eerie light in her palm. She raised her eyes to Ram. "How could that be? How—who is he, Ram?"

"I don't know. Nor do I know from where he came except—except I'm beginning to imagine he came from a distance farther than any place we know."

"Then will we not see him again? He—I trusted him, Ram. He was—I thought he was very special."

"Special? Yes, very special. With talents I have not mastered, Telien. But, see him again? I don't know." He looked down at her and a shiver touched him, of cold terrible wonder. If either of them were to see Anchorstar again, *where* would they see him? In what time would they see him? If Telien were to see him—he touched her hair and felt again that heart-rending fear for her.

When at last the prisoners were mounted, Telien kept herself apart from them, pulled her pony aside and held back to Ram. He touched her pack, tied behind the saddle. "You carry food, Telien. But there is food in plenty in the wagon. And this pony . . ."

"He is a sturdy pony for the mountains, Ram. I do not follow the rest."

His heart lifted. "Do you mean you ride with me, then, into the valley of Eresu?"

"No, Ramad. You go where you are needed, and I must do the same. The mare will need me. She will need salves until her wings are healed, care the stallion cannot give her. She will need, very soon now, tending while she bears her foal, which no stallion, no matter how wise, can give her. I will follow Meheegan into the mountains."

He took her hand, held the lantern up. "Still you do not remember the thunder, the shaking earth."

"I remember nothing such as that. How can I remember something that has not happened to me?" Her eyes were huge, very green. "I'll tell you this, Ramad of wolves. If that memory has to do with you, if it is something we should remember together, then I promise you I would never forget it."

Ram reached to touch her cheek, said without understanding his own words until after he had spoken them, "If you do not remember, Telien, then—then that which I remember has . . . not yet happened to you."

They stared at each other perplexed, and Ram went cold with the knowledge of what he had said. Time, for Telien, was *yet* to warp. The sense of her being swept away from him in Time was yet to happen. Yes, all of it, waiting for her somewhere in Time itself, as a crouching animal waits. What would happen to her after those few moments in Tala-charen? What would the warping of

Time do to her then? He could not let her go, could not part from her now, knowing not when she would be swept away; when or if he would see her again.

She saw his fear for her and could not ask, saw that he would have her stay. She leaned and kissed him. "I—I will be in the mountains when—when you come to me." There were tears on her cheeks. She swung her horse around suddenly and broke it into a gallop up through the muddy camp in the direction the mare had gone.

He turned, grabbed the reins of a saddled horse, had his foot in the stirrup when he stopped himself, stood staring after her with a new feeling, a feeling he would not have for another.

He had no right to stop her because of his fear for her, because of his own need for her. She must do what was needed. But part of him was with her, would always be with her. He tied the horse, turned away desolate, turned to getting the captives started on their journey home.

He chose three men to ride south to intercept Jerthon. The rest of the band set out at once straight for Blackcob. Ere's two moons had lifted free of cloud at last, to hang like slim scythes. With their light, the band would make good time. Two men remained in Kubal to meet the small band from the north and to dish out gruel to the penned prisoners, the soldiers of AgWurt. Once the two had left, releasing the prisoners, not a horse would remain in Kubal, not a weapon save one or two for hunting meat.

At last Ram headed out north, up toward the source of the river Urobb, for there, so the old tales told, so inscriptions in the caves of the gods told, he would find Eresu.

Alone in the night, Telien was stricken with a terrible longing for Ram. She tried with difficulty to keep her thoughts to guessing which way the mare might have gone. With AgWurt dead, Meheegan might well return to the cloistered, grass-rich valley in spite of her memory of the snare. Telien headed north through the land that AgWurt had taken from murdered settlers. Now that he was dead, could his men hold this land? AgWurt, dead—because of his own cruelty and blood lust. And for the first time since her mother had died when she was very small, Telien felt the sudden light, free sense of wholeness that comes with the absence of fear.

Nothing she could face in these mountains, nothing in the night or in all of Ere itself could make her afraid in the way she had feared AgWurt. She was suddenly made of light; she lay her reins on her mount's neck and stretched her arms upward into the cold night, stretched her body up and felt the last harness of fear slip away as if she lifted herself into a world she had forgotten existed.

And she thought of Ram, now, with joy. No matter the future, her life was remade with Ram's. How could you know someone so short a time yet feel you had belonged together forever? She spoke his name into the night like a litany, "Ram. Ramad of wolves." An immensity of space seemed to surround Ram, the very air around him to break into fragments that revealed a world beyond, revealed wonders and freedom she could hardly imagine. The freedom of Carriol was a part of it, but more than that: a freedom of spirit such as she had never known. There would be no lies with Ram. If there were pain and danger, they would know these things together. She would accept pain gladly now, so that Ram should not bear it alone.

In the hills south of Kubal, most of Jerthon's battalion slept soundly, their heads couched on saddles, their bows and swords close beside them—colder companions than women but sometimes steadier. Jerthon, riding guard, saw the signal fire first. It flared three times, then twice, then three. Ram's signal. Jerthon and the other three who rode guard woke the battalion to saddle up, then all sat their fidgeting horses waiting to see what would come down out of the hills. Maybe Ram. Maybe something else. The journey through Folkstone had been strange, with dark, unsettling winds and a heavy blackness sweeping the stars above them, then gone; and something unseen running through the woods jibbering so the horses were strung tight with fear.

They waited in silence, the horses restive. The night wind had stilled and the cold increased. At last they could make out a rider moving down toward them, then another, finally could see three riders. And then Emern's voice came suddenly, Emern who had been captive of the Kubalese; Emern's voice light and questioning on the cold night air. "Captain? Is it Jerthon?"

"Yes! Great Eresu, man, where have you come from? Who rides with you?"

"Cald and Lorden, Captain!"

They rode down fast, their horses sliding and blowing. The three men leaped from their saddles to be embraced by their fellows and by Jerthon. "Shadows of Urdd!" Jerthon bellowed, "How did you get free? Where are the rest?"

He had the story quickly and with confusion from the three of them, how Ram had come captive into Kubal, how the stallion of Eresu had killed AgWurt. Ram had then ridden off into the mountains and the rest of the captives headed straight for Blackcob. The elation among Jerthon's troops was as wild as if foxes danced, and a jug was passed, then soon enough the battalion was heading for home double-time across the night hills; and all of them knowing they would meet their comrades and brothers and wives safe in Carriol. They rode hard and forded the Urobb near dawn to come onto Carriol land, the narrow valley that marked her western border.

Strange that no herd animals could be seen, for the herds grazed heavily here. At the first farmhouse they found all the animals crowded into barn and sheds, gates locked. They approached the house, saw it was shuttered and bolted.

Jerthon dismounted and approached the door, bow drawn. A tiny opening in the door was bared, a face looked out, and then the door was thrown open and Jerthon could see the farmer's family inside blinking in the sudden light like a bunch of owls; and they had nine young colts in there with them corralled between cots and table. He stood staring in, wondering if the whole tribe had gone mad. Old Midden Herm, the patriarch, said gruffly, "Something came here, Captain. Something dark and wild is come down out of the sky."

Jerthon stared at Midden. "Out of the sky?"

"Yes, Seer. Out of the sky. Something dark and huge as the clouds and so fast you never see it. It is there and gone, and the animals lay stripped of flesh where they stood." He led Jerthon out and showed him five horses' skeletons stripped clean, scattered on the turf. "You see the darkness come, the wind goes wild, you see the dark that is its shadow maybe. It is all screaming wind, then it is gone and the horses are like that." Midden stood staring sickly at the scattered bones. "Like that, Seers. Our animals—our poor animals."

Jerthon put his arm around the old man. He had worked so hard with the breeding, had taken such care with the selection of a stallion, with the nurturing of the mares and the careful, gentle training of the colts. He felt the old man's sickness as his own at this mindless destruction.

Mindless? Was it mindless?

"And the dark—the thing of dark moves eastward, Seer. Toward the ruins."

Jerthon and his troops rode fast then to the east, pounding hard across the early morning hills, arrived on sweating, blowing horses to find the town shuttered and bolted just as Midden's farm had been. Every house and shop closed tight. No animal to be seen, no person.

He stared up at the citadel and saw that the portals had been covered with the slabs of stone that slid across from within.

THE COUNCIL and the townsfolk all had gathered in the citadel, sealed the portals, had chambered the horses and cattle in the lower caves and sealed these portals, too, as the invisible dark murmured and swept round the tower.

At last the council drew together and began to make its way down stone flights toward the main portal that led to the town. Skeelie stared at Drudd's broad back where he marched before her and thought she had never been this afraid, even in Burgdeeth. Behind her, behind Pol and the others, the people of Carriol crowded down the stairs too, all of them armed. And in front of Skeelie, Tayba held the runestone. Their minds—their every strength—were linked to it to create one power against the dark; and beyond the portals as they descended, the dark creature screamed out its fury, and it descended too, its great maw lusting after flesh. At the far end of the deserted town, Jerthon and his battalion came silently, walking their sweating, spent horses in between the farthest cottages.

And neither group of Seers touched the thoughts of the other, each blinded in silence by the dark; and the dark increased until morning was as night. And creatures began to be born from the dark, horned, slithering creatures that swept the blackened sky with leathery wings then descended without sound onto the thatched rooftops and began to creep in silence down the stone walls.

In the portal, the runestone glowed in Tayba's hands as the Seers' powers gathered, as slowly they tried to force the creature of dark back, to force half-seen monsters back and back into darkness; but still the dark advanced: their powers were not enough.

Without, the dark creatures lurched and faded, became winds raging. Became, then, a part of the sea, so waves lashed in fury upon the tower seeking to break it away. The sea pounded in tidal humpings against the lower caves, and they filled with rushing water then drained, then filled again and the frantic cattle and horses swam in the cave blindly and in terror, and the weakest among them drowned.

The runestone shone with the power of the Seers as Tayba held it high, battling the wind and the raging sea, battling the dark with every fiber she possessed. Then as Jerthon came closer, the dark swept down in the form of a huge bird-monster, silently above him, changeable as wind, brother to wind, and clawed, with great beak reaching; he did not sense it; it dropped low over Jerthon's band and followed them, invisible to them, as the battalion came through the narrow streets in darkness knowing there was danger but blinded to its source, every man's weapon drawn. The sweating horses cowed in fear as unseen creatures shadowed them and crouched waiting among houses and shops.

Tayba saw Jerthon come, a sudden glimpse, tried to cry out to him and could not, tried to run through the streets to him and couldn't move, was held as if she were stone, and her voice would not come in her throat.

What was this power come so strong out of Pelli? She pushed at her dark hair with quaking hand as if it would stifle her; her every fiber strained, yet no sound or forward movement could she make, and when she turned she saw Drudd's fury—did he think she wasn't trying? Did he think—she stared at Pol, white beneath his freckles, at Skeelie, her thin face drawn with effort; then she turned back and felt the dark descending around Jerthon, and she tore with her very soul at it, with a will close to hysteria against the surging dark.

There stood in the heart of the Pellian nation a wood of ancient twisted trees so dense the air beneath did not know sun; a wood so old it had seen the first coming of men into Ere; a wood chill of spirit as death is chill. No one ventured there save the Pellian Seers. In the center of the wood rose a black stone wall, and inside this wall the Pellians had wrought a castle, grotesque in design, shaped like the joined heads of a snake, an eel, and a horned man, their grinning mouths serving as high portals, their eyes leering windows. And a creature lived within the castle, a creature named Hape. This was the castle of Hape.

Below the three grinning heads that formed the upper castle ran three rows of windows narrow and dark, and beneath these again was an arched place whose door was carven with the Hape's runes and with signs of death and adversity.

At first, three years earlier, the Hape had been no more than a whispering dark reaching from beyond the mountains to summon BroogArl. Heeding its call, BroogArl had sent Seers north into the dark mountains to seek the Hape out, an expedition that traveled past the gods' city of Owdneet, past the mountain Tala-charen, and past Eresu itself, far, far into the unknown places, led on by the Hape's soft urging: twelve Seers and apprentice Seers traveling two years, and returning at last to Pelli not alone. The Hape rode with them, rode the winds above them, nurtured on their dark thoughts as they traveled, and grew stronger than ever it had been. It ran beside their shying horses as a great six-legged cat, or it strode beside their cringing mounts as a giant with head of goat and deer's horns; or it housed itself in the dark of their minds only and rode there. When the Seers arrived in Pelli, it housed itself in the castle they built for it at its own instruction, and BroogArl knew he had captured a creature of evil beyond his wildest dreams. There in the wood, Hape would come out at night in the shape of a horned man or an eel or snake, or in the form of a thousand chittering creatures slithering unseen. This was Hape, potent, feeding on the dark Seers' minds and nurturing at their evil wills, slave to their wills—or was he slave?

Who ruled now? The Seers of Pelli, or Hape?

Perhaps it did not matter who ruled in this coupling of evil.

The Gods

Chapter Six

ERE'S THIN MOONS lit Ram's way from Kubal toward the River Urobb; then he rode up along the fast-falling moonlit river, atop a ridge, toward the first jagged peaks of the Ring of Fire; rode, knowing that beneath those cold stone peaks the mountains' bellies burned with molten fire tenuously contained, boiling rivers fettered now, but always eager to be free. All of Ere lived with this sense of the mountains' captive fire; it was a part of Ere's race-memory, the knowledge that the land might suddenly burst forth in rivers of fire. Such knowledge should have made Ere's men close and kind with one another, but it never had.

As he rode, his vision cleared suddenly without warning in a way he could never understand. What made the dark leaders pull back of a sudden, so that those of light could see? Were their powers amassed elsewhere, and thus weakened for a few moments in the blocking of other Seers' skills? He Saw the Hape suddenly and clearly, saw what it was and how the Seer BroogArl had brought it into Ere less than a year past, saw the Hape's dark lust, saw the castle that was built for it. He pulled up his horse, turned, sat staring back through the night toward Pelli, the vision holding him. And he understood at last what the power was they had been battling, remembered Jerthon's voice in citadel, "Something rides with them, Ram.

Something more than the dark we know, something like an impossible weight on your mind so the Seeing is torn from you, your very sanity near torn from you . . ." He remembered his own feelings in battle, his words to Skeelie as she tended his wound, "A power that breathes and moves as one great lusting animal . . ."

It *was* an animal, this breath of evil that BroogArl had brought out of the unknown lands, a monster not of flesh but formed of hatred and lust.

He went on at last, shaken by the dark vision, afraid of it, and awed.

Toward morning he made camp high up a ridge, dozed over a small fire as his horse grazed, then came awake suddenly with a sharp sense of something amiss and saw the moon had set and in the east the sun was already casting its light across the far sea. What had waked him? He sat staring at his dozing mount and slowly, coldly, he began to sense a heaviness: a peril over Carriol. He felt the dark's attack then, and in confusion, nothing clear, tried to See in a sharper vision and could not, but was gripped with a terrifying sense of disaster.

When at last the vision went from him, he did not know whether the dark had drawn away from Carriol in defeat, or whether Carriol lay defeated. Should he go back, should he ride for Carriol?

But that would be useless, he could not arrive in time. He strained to use his power against the evil monster and could touch nothing, was as blind. He turned desperately and saddled up, rode quickly up the ridge; perhaps if he were in Eresu his power would come stronger, so he could help. He rode hard and was soon deep in a zantha wood where the leaves hung down like a woman's hair, trailing tendrils wet from the night dew, drenching him.

He came out of the wood at long last to ride up along the Urobb until he found a shallow fording with a vein of smooth white stone skirting the other side. He forded here and followed that smooth trail quickly, with growing urgency.

He came at midmorning to a narrow, dark canyon with twisting black boulders rising against its walls, a place immensely silent, where his horse's hoofbeats fell like blows. The land rose steeply, soon was too abrupt and rocky for any horse. Here Ram unsaddled the gelding and turned him loose, leaned his saddle inside a shallow cave out of the weather, shouldered his pack, and started ahead on foot up beside the fast-falling river.

The way grew narrower and steeper still, and distant rumblings began to speak inside the mountains. The sun was high when he came suddenly around boulders to where the river ended abruptly and he stood facing a barrier, facing the sheer rocky wall of a mountain.

The river vanished beneath the mountain; or rather, came flowing out from beneath it in a clear swirl. The water should have been dark but was not, was washed with light as if light itself flowed out from beneath the stone. The old songs spoke of just such a swirling pool washed with light, of the river's end lighted from beyond: from Eresu. He began to search the mountain's face for a way to enter into that fabled valley.

He could find no opening among the boulders and crevices, there was no cleft that might lead him through into the valley. As he searched, the mountains to the west rumbled again, spoke long trembling oaths deep inside their bellies, so he was distracted with sudden fear for Telien. He continued to search, but could see clearly only Telien's face, was distraught thinking of her danger if the mountains exploded in fire.

He had no sense of being watched, no normal Seer's quickening to the sense of another observing him, so skilled was the Seer who stood half-hidden in shadow against the stone cliff. When at last the figure stirred, lifted a hand, Ram started violently.

The man, sun-browned against brown stone, clad in brown robes like the stone, was hardly visible. When he moved, calling attention to himself, Ram stared, startled, drew his sword in reflex so its tip touched the tall man's belly; but he stared into the face of the tall Seer, felt the sense of him, and lowered his sword, grinning almost sheepishly. This man meant him no harm. He was—he was as pure and unsullied as if he were himself a sort of god. Ram stood with lowered sword studying the man. He was old, his face thin and lined, his nose very prominent. The lid of one eye drooped. His beard and locks were stained with a ruddy hue that must once have been red as Ram's own, but was pale now.

Ram knew at once the man's name was Pender, knew he had come here to guide him; knew, with sudden shyness, that the gods waited his coming, felt utterly ignorant suddenly, as inept as a baby, leaden-tongued. So close to the gods now. So close. Felt a sudden fear of going on; but he must go on, and quickly. Must, when he entered Eresu, turn all his power to helping the battle in Carriol before ever he could turn to another mission.

The old man, watching him, said suddenly and abruptly, "Try now, Ramad. I will show you, help you." And Pender gave him, with sudden jolting clarity, a vision of the battle in Carriol, so powerful a vision that Ram felt the grim determination of the Seers as they battled the Hape. He held the wolf bell, felt his own force grow within him; saw the runestone glowing in Tayba's hands. He reached out with the council to try to turn the dark, saw silent creatures slithering among buildings, saw Jerthon's battalion and the dark monster flying above them, its claws outstretched like knives; then saw Jerthon's men fighting it, and his spirit fought beside them. Saw blood flow and terrified horses rearing and falling as the Hape swung low on buzzard wings, saw Skeelie start forward, and Tayba grab her wrist. Men and women were streaming out of the tower to do battle with the Hape. Ram was with them, felt the Seers' total strength forcing upon the monster, the power of the stone like fire; felt the Hape unbalancing at last; saw Jerthon's soldiers strike and slash as its beating wings struck them, its beak struck them; their horses were wild, cringing down, spinning and falling. Riders leaped clear, swords flashing. Ram saw Jerthon kick his mount into submission as he thrust sword again and again at the bird-Hape, at the dark beak and neck, and Ram thrust with him—until at last the Seers' powers began to weaken the Hape and confuse it, and for a moment its senses went awry:

A silent moment, the forces balanced. But then the Hape's powers surged stronger in a last dying frenzy, and suddenly it was three-headed, the horned cat's head lashing out with teeth like knives, the man's head laughing, the eel's head tearing a soldier's face; but the heads even as they battled weakened in the strength of their images, came and went in clarity and vigor as the creature clawed at the horses so they fell stumbling among their fellows on bloodstained cobbles. The Hape rose surging with fury as the soldiers beat it back, it was mad with their attack now, flung men like toys as others cut and flailed its body. In the portal of the tower, the silent council of Seers hardly breathed in their terrible concentration, and the powers balanced, tilted—Ram brought his own power stronger, sweating, calling the power of the wolf bell; buoying the power of the Seers until at last the Hape weakened again, wavered, swung low in the air. Soldiers grabbed its wings, pulled it down; it thrashed, then it was suddenly wingless, was only a snake writhing and lashing among them, the leathery wings they had pinnioned quite gone. They fell on it, striking steel blows, crowding it in their fury until it turned away screaming—but it carried the body of a man in its jaws.

It moved fast, thrashing, crowded on all sides by hard-riding soldiers, would not drop the screaming man, lunged out between buildings toward freedom.

But it was dying, writhed twisting in death as it fled. It lay still at last, in a field, the wounded soldier crumpled in its jaws, the soldiers' swords thick in it as quills, their spent horses resting over it, blowing. And behind them all of Carriol advanced, horses foaming in fear, men and women on foot with weapons raised. The Seers, Ram, brought every power they possessed down through the runestone then, to destroy it utterly.

But it was not destroyed utterly. Suddenly the Hape was no animal but only an essence of dark, a shapeless darkness growing thinner and thinner until grass could be seen through patches of melting hide and blood. And then it was not there, was only a blowing blackness on the wind. Hape was the wind, was a darkness flung between earth and cloud.

The Hape had fled, and the soldier lay dead on the grass, his blood drying in the cold sun.

Ram saw less clearly now, as in a dream. Saw Skeelie running through the bloody streets to embrace her brother, Saw people surging out of the tower to tend the wounded. Saw Seers' white robes smeared with blood, women and children kneeling over bodies. He saw Tayba standing alone in the portal holding the runestone in her shaking hands, saw Jerthon look up at her across half the town, his green eyes kindling, saw him go to her striding through blood, past wounded men and animals, past Skeelie, hardly seeing her. Jerthon leaped the three steps to the portal and took Tayba in his arms. Ram felt Jerthon's love for her, and he felt her fear and trembling and her uncertainty.

Chapter Six

Ram stood for a long time after the vision faded. So strong a vision. His gaze returned to Pender, to the drooping eye, the thin, lined face. "And," Ram said, choking, "what—what of Telien?"

"Telien—Telien I cannot show you," Pender said. "You have no need, she must find her own way among the Ring of Fire. And you must abide, Ramad of wolves. Now you have seen the Hape at last, Ramad. Would you defeat the Hape?"

"I would, Pender. How—But can *I* defeat it?"

"Only you, Ramad of Zandour, only you can answer that." The old man scratched his chin briefly. "And if you do not defeat it, what of Carriol, of Ere?" Pender turned without waiting for an answer and led Ram up along a nearly invisible ledge and into a crevice behind outcroppings of stone.

They entered into absolute darkness, continued to climb, and rose at last into an underground cave lighted from above by an opening where the sun stood flaring down.

Beneath their feet was an immense slab of stone hollowed underneath by the river, the river flowed beneath them into a triangular pool reflecting perfectly the high noon sun.

The cave walls were carved into wavelike shapes by long past action of the river, and the river's flow now cast the sun's flicking light back upon these, so the whole cave seemed to be moving underwater. A memory came sharp to Ram, of another cave filled with light, and he was nine years old; he and Skeelie stripped naked were swimming in just such a light-struck pool, in a cave in the old city of Owdneet. Pender turned to look at him.

"The Luff'Eresi await you, Ramad. They would hear you plead your mission." Then he turned, led Ram in silence toward the back of the cave and through a high opening into a second, larger cave more brightly sunwashed still, and Ram saw far mountains beyond the portal and went forward to the brink of the drop, stared out upon a valley immense and green, so far below that it took his breath.

Below him, perhaps half a mile, the valley floor rolled in green fields and gentle hills and small copses of feathery trees. A river wound through, and across the valley in the cliffs that formed the opposite wall were caves, a city of caves one above the other in clusters, with balconies and windows, and some with steps leading one to another; though no steps led down to the valley so far below.

And then he saw the light shifting and changing in the valley as if something were there. Yes, winged figures barely visible in slanting light among the valleys and hills, shifting and indistinct as light on running water, iridescent shapes moving in and out of his vision, ephemeral as dreams, ever moving, ever flashing against the solid background of hills and cliffs. The Luff'Eresi were there, their images as elusive and compelling as music.

And suddenly near to him, filling the air before him, came the horses of Eresu, not light-washed like the gods, but solid, familiar animals crowding out of the sky to land around Ram and Pender, warm, familiar animals dropping their feathered wings across their backs as they entered the cave, pushing around Ram and Pender with great good humor, nickering, nudging them with velvet muzzles. A gray stallion knelt in the accustomed invitation to mount and took Ram on his back, stood at the brink of the cave, his wings flaring around Ram, catching wind; and they were airborne suddenly, sweeping down toward the valley so the rush of air took Ram's breath. He turned to see Pender close behind; they swept low over the valley, and Ram could see the light-washed Luff'Eresi now, see a few clusters of white robed men and women, too, and understood from Pender that, all through time, some few Seers had come into Eresu for sanctuary from the harsher world of Ere.

Horses of Eresu were grazing on the hills. Some leaped skyward now and again in bucking play. Ram watched a dozen colts run across a hill to launch themselves clumsily into the wind, flapping and fighting for height. Some dropped down in defeat, but two lifted onto the wind at last, kicking and bucking.

The silver stallion descended, and below, the Luff'-Eresi were gathered and waiting. Ram looked with surprise, for there were females among the Luff'Eresi, women's shapely forms rising from the softer curves of mare's bodies. He felt the ripple of amusement stir among the Luff'Eresi at his amazement, felt Pender's silent laughter. Had he thought the Luff'Eresi were of one sex and did not reproduce themselves?

Yes, he realized, he had thought just that, had believed the Luff'Eresi immortal in spite of his childhood reasoning that they were not. In his most private self he must have believed the Luff'Eresi immortal—or have wanted to believe this—for reproduction and birth, and thus dying, had never been a part of how he pictured them.

Their voices rang like a shout in his mind. *Yes, we are mortal, Ramad of wolves!* Their laughter rocked him. *Mortal just as you! Not gods! Never gods!*

The gray stallion landed on the grassy turf in a rush of wind and bid Ram remain on his back. Ram saw that even mounted he had to look up to the Luff'Eresi. From the ground he would have been a tiny creature indeed, staring upward to face the two dozen winged gods. No, *not* gods! But it would take him a while to get used to that idea. And, if they were not gods, what made them shimmer and seem to shift in space so they could not be clearly seen?

We dwell on a different plane, Ramad of Zandour. We live among the valleys and mountains of your dimension, but our dimension is different. So you do not see us clearly. You percieve us as we percieve you, as through a changing curtain of light-struck air. It is because of this, in part, that we have been thought gods. But we are not gods, we are mortal just as you.

"If you are not gods, then those of Carriol who pray to you . . ." he broke off. The beauty of the Luff'Eresi stirred a wonder in him so he wanted only to stare, to memorize every line, the lean, smooth equine bodies so much more beautifully made than horses, the clean lines of the human torsos more perfect than the bodies of men. Their expressions, their whole demeanor was of such joy, it was as if they found in life the very essence of joy, found pleasure and meaning that men had not yet learned to perceive. As if they had no time for the small, trivial unpleasantnesses of men, no time or patience for evil and its ways.

"If you are not gods," he repeated, "then those who pray are praying to—a lie." His words shocked him. He felt the wrongness of this and the discomfort it caused them. But he needed to know, he needed to sort it out.

We are not gods, Ramad, but there is a power higher than we, and prayers are heard—heard not by gods or by anything like gods, as men imagine them. Heard simply by a higher level of power. There was distant thunder then, but the Luff'Eresi seemed not to heed it. Dark formless clouds—or was it smoke?—lay above the western peaks.

There are lives on many planes, Ramad of wolves, and powers in many degrees. Beyond this world our lives would seem as the lives of ants. Life is planes above planes, power above power.

Ram understood more clearly through the sense of it they gave him, than through words. Understood within himself quite suddenly the power that linked all life, touched each living being. *Those who pray can touch it, Ramad, just as we touch it now as we speak to you. A Seer touches that power each time he reaches out.* Ram saw, more clearly then than he ever would afterward, layers of life stretched out one then another through all space and time, and he understood the wonder of being born again, and again, into new lives.

Born again, Ramad, provided one equips himself to be reborn. If he does not, if he has created evil, or nurtured evil with his way of life, if he has sucked upon the misery and pain of others, then he goes not forward into new lives but dies and turns to dust.

It is the choice of each. But that, Ramad, is not why you come to us. Now that you know that the children who burn in Venniver's fire will likely be born anew to a higher power, do you still wish to pursue your quest?

Ram stared at the tall winged being who had come forward and stood close to him, his color like light over gold, his torso bronzed, his eyes deep and seeing, compelling. He thought about children dying by fire and could feel their pain. He understood too clearly that what he desired was against all the Luff'Eresi believed. That to change the lives of men was to destroy that which men had woven of their web of survival and of learning. To take away one evil from that web was to *act* as gods in altering men's lives. He understood that this would weaken man, that man could be strengthened only by altering his own fate. But again he felt the pain and fear of children dying by fire, and he could not let that rest. "Yes," he said at last. "I wish to pursue my quest. I wish to beg your help for the children, to beg you once to touch the lives of men and change them. Will turning aside one evil destroy all of Ere? Venniver will not be destroyed, only discouraged from killing. The Seeing children, the Children of Ynell, can then survive to destroy him as they should. If those children do not survive, the power that fights against Venniver will be crippled perhaps beyond all hope.

"Without your help in turning Venniver aside from this destruction, the only other course is for Carriol to march into Burgdeeth and destroy her," Ram said quietly. "And I do not know, with the dark so strong, with the powers against us at this moment so great, whether Carriol can destroy both Burgdeeth and Pelli. And we must, at all costs, destroy Pelli. Destroy the Hape, before it places all of Ere under its will. Burgdeeth—the Seers of Burgdeeth can survive if only a measure of fear is laid down upon Venniver. Something to prevent his senseless killing. We need you now, we need this one thing of you—in the name of freedom. In the name of kindness and love for those who are imprisoned."

Do you ask it, then?

"I ask it. In the name of the innocent who suffer. In the name of the Children, those skilled above all others, who might bring great glory upon Ere if they are but given this one chance, this one small shift in Ere's path of dark, I ask that you help us."

The Luff'Eresi smiled, shifted; light flashed around them so Ram could not be sure they were still there. Then he could see them once more, iridescent, leaping skyward so quickly he could only stare. They were leaving him, they would not help; then suddenly the gray stallion leaped to join them, wings shattering wind, nearly unseating Ram. He was airborne suddenly, flying up over Eresu among the Luff'Eresi in one swift climb, and the Luff'Eresi said in his mind with one voice, *So be it, Ramad of the wolves. You have had the courage to come to us, to ask of us when you doubted we would help you. So it is the doing of one man, of a man's caring, that turns the scale. One man, Ramad, has thus laid his change upon Ere.*

Ram frowned, puzzling. "But that would mean—that anyone could come to you. With any kind of . . ."

No! They thundered. *It is a matter of commitment, Ramad, a matter of truth, of the true right to ask. But Ramad*

. . . and their voices were as one in his mind . . . *the deception upon Venniver must be done our way. And you may not like that way. You will be our decoy, Ramad. It will be you, Ramad of Zandour, Venniver's old enemy, who will stand tied to the stake in Venniver's temple waiting to die by fire.*

Ram swallowed, felt a sudden emptiness in the pit of his stomach as if the stallion had dropped sharply in the sky.

Have you faith enough in our word to do as we direct you, Ramad of wolves?

He looked around him at the glinting, light-filled figures, huge, filling the sky around him so their wings overlapped in a torrent of shattering light. He felt the immensity of their minds, of their spirits, an immensity beyond any of man's petty concerns. He swallowed again, said without question, "Yes. I have faith. I will do as you direct. I would . . ." and he paused, wanting to be very sure he spoke truly. "I would, if it were needed, die to free those who are captive of Venniver." And a sense of death filled him suddenly and utterly, and with it the sense of Telien, of her face, her cool green eyes; a sudden longing for her twisted and held him as nothing in his life ever had.

They moved fast over jagged peaks. Below, a gray stain of smoke rose to tear apart on the wind. A faint rumble stirred the air. The mountains were speaking; and again, with their voices, Ram's fear for Telien came cold and sharp.

Could the dark be making the mountains stir? Did the dark have power enough, now, to draw fire from the very mountains? He was clutching the stallion's mane, his palms sweating. Well, but the red stallion was with Telien, he could fly with her clear of sudden disaster—if he *would* fly clear, if he would leave his mare to perish. Or would the red stallion prefer to die with Meheegan, and so let Telien die?

Chapter Seven

Telien knelt beside the mare, rubbing dolba salve into the poor, swollen legs. The passage up the mountain had been hard on Meheegan, the weight of the unborn foal slowing her. The winged ones' legs were not made for hard treks over stone and uneven ways, for climbing rocky cliffs. The mare watched her, head down, her breath warm on Telien's neck, the relief she felt at Telien's attention very clear.

Telien had followed blindly after the mare and stallion, could only guess where they might go, had come to the valley near dawn and found it empty, had stared uncertainly out over the emerging black ridges against the dawn-streaked sky, wondering if she had been a fool to think she could find them in these vast, wild mountains. She had scanned the bare peaks not knowing which way to take or what to do, wondering if she should turn back, when suddenly she had seen them high on a ridge making their way slowly up along the side of a mountain. She had galloped after them eagerly, had come upon them at last to find the mare so spent she could not go farther, unable to get down into the sharp ravine where the stallion had found water for her. Telien had carried water in her waterskin, tipping it out into her cupped hand so the mare could drink; then she had doctored Meheegan's wings where the tender skin had rubbed against stone until it bled. Now she rubbed in the cooling salve, smoothed it into the mare's swollen legs, then watched as the mare went off slowly to find a patch of grass between boulders.

The stallion came to nudge Meheegan softly, caress her; then at last he, too, began to graze. Telien's own mount ate hungrily where she had hobbled him. He stared at the mare and stallion sometimes with a look of terrible curiosity, but he did not like to be near them.

Telien made camp simply by spreading her blanket beneath an outcrop of stone. She drank some water, chewed absently on a bit of mountain meat as the afternoon light dimmed into evening. The immensity of the mountains was a wonder to her. She had lived all her life at their feet and never once climbed up into them. AgWurt would not have allowed such a thing. To slip away to the hill meadows was one thing, but to go as far as the mountains, that long journey, and not be found out had been impossible. But these dark peaks stirred her, she wanted to share this with Ram; she imagined his voice, close, so she shivered. *You do not remember the thunder and the shaking earth?* Then, *If you do not remember, then that which I remember has not yet happened to you.* Not yet happened? She lay in her blanket puzzling, but it made no sense to her. She *wanted* to remember, she wanted—her caring made her tremble with its intensity. They had been meant always for each other, the separation of their early lives had been a mistake of fate only now made right.

She was so tired. Dreaming of Ram, she turned her face to the mountain and slept, slept straight through the night and deep into the morning, woke with the sun full in her face and the thunder of the mountains harsh all around her. She stared across at the stallion, his wings lifted involuntarily as instinct made him yearn skyward, his nostrils distended, his ears sharp forward, his eyes white-edged. He blew softly toward the mare. Her head was up, staring wildly. Telien shivered, her mind filled suddenly with tales of burning lava flowing over the lands. And where was Ram, was he safe from the flow of fire? Ram—alone somewhere deep within the mountains. Ramad . . .

She did not see the winged ones passing high above her, did not see the glancing swirl of light made by the Luff'Eresi in motion, nor see the one winged stallion, silver gray, carrying a rider above her across Ere's winds.

Suddenly she remembered, for no reason, her father's face in death and was chilled, very alone. He had been a cold, unbending master who beat her, who tortured helpless creatures before her for the pleasure of seeing her distress. The powerful, mindless threat of the mountains was not like AgWurt's purposeful threats; though the mountains could destroy her just as easily as ever AgWurt might have.

THE WINDS SWEPT and leaped around Ram, the gray stallion's wings sang on the wind; on all sides the flying Luff'Eresi shone as if the stallion beat through a river of shattering light. Below, the jagged peaks lay brutal as death. Along a dark ridge Ram could see smoke rising in wind-borne gusts. He thought of Telien with sharp, sudden clarity, with a harsh longing, as above the wind came the rumble of shifting earth, speaking of fires deep within. Ram's fear for her was terrible. But the Luff'Eresi laughed, a roaring, thundering mirth of great good will, and one swept so close to Ram his light-washed wings seemed to twine with the stallion's feathered wings. He said his name to Ram, and it was not a word to be spoken but a handful of musical notes cutting across the wind. *She will be hurt and afraid, Ramad. But there is likelihood she will live.*

"Can't you *stop* the fires!" Ram shouted. "Can't you make a safe way for her! She . . ."

The Luff'Eresi roared in his mind, *Cannot! We cannot do such a thing! And it is not the right of any of us to ask Telien to abandon what she is about. You must abide, Ramad! And no creature of Ere can stop a tantrum of nature! Men—simple men, Ramad—believe we make the fires. We do not do that, no more than are we gods! To think we are gods makes men feel safe, for that is easier to understand than to try to understand our differences. And men think we make the fires because that is the easiest thing to believe. But men grow, Ramad. They believe, then they question that belief. They find a new truth, then question again. They come at last, by a long painful route, to real truth. And that truth, Ramad, is more shot with wonder than ever was the myth.*

Ram looked around at the light-washed bodies moving on the wind, so alien to him yet so right. "How does . . ." he began, and felt very young and unsure. "How does man know the truth when at last he finds it, then? How does he, when he thinks each belief is truth?"

The Luff'Eresi's laugh was a windswept roar. *He proves it, Ramad. At each belief man finds ways to think he proves that belief. At last one day he will understand how to find real proof, to look at the small, minute parts of a thing and understand its nature from that. Even then, Ramad, even when he is able to prove, man will only see the beginning of proof and think that is everything.*

Ram puzzled over this and stored it away to ponder at a later time, felt awed by the thoughts it began to awaken within him. He could see Kubal now, off to his left, lit by the dropping sun. He turned, stared back toward the eastern mountains and saw smoke rising there and a stream of red lava winding down toward the Voda Cul, for there in the east, too, a mountain had erupted. Twisting around, holding a handful of mane to steady himself, he stared out beneath Dalwyn's lifting wings to see five peaks spaced around the rim of the Ring of Fire, spewing smoke: all along the ring, then, some great underground force was belching up. He turned back, looked toward Carriol. The ruins did not seem threatened, nor the loess plains in the north. Blackcob, farther west, was the only part of Carriol that lay directly below the fires, and even there the lava was well to the north of her. Carriol's coast lay untouched, softened in mists that rose from the sea. He longed for the peace of his cave room, with the rippling sea light washing across its ceiling, the roar of the sea like a second heartbeat. He imagined Telien there, then turned away from that thought.

They were past the mountains now and above the foothills near Burgdeeth. Ram leaned across the stallion's neck to stare down at the grassy, empty hills, and at the great desert plain south beyond Burgdeeth that brought sharp memories. He had fled from the Seer HarThass's apprentice across that plain, he and Tayba, he a child of eight, and Tayba caught willingly in HarThass's web so she had nearly got him killed.

The stallion landed between rocky knolls, but the Luff' Eresi remained skyborne like a bright, swirling cloud above him. *We leave you here, Ramad of wolves, but we will return. Now go you into Burgdeeth. Become Venniver's captive there—if you believe in us, if you trust us to return, if you believe in what you want of us. Go, and allow yourself to be taken.*

Ram slid down from the stallion's back. The Luff' Eresi disappeared in a surge of iridescent light, were gone utterly; the sky was clear once more, unfractured by light, as if all matter had returned to its customary and familiar place in the world, mundane and lonely. A whole dimension had been suddenly removed, a dimension ultimately desirable. Ram stood with the stallion in the strange, lonely calm, rubbing the sleek, silvery neck. Then at last the gray horse leaped away too, to slip across winds. Ram watched him disappear, flying easterly away from Burgdeeth so he would not be seen from that place. He stared up at the mountains, stricken with a great emptiness, suddenly very much alone.

Smoke rose above the mountains like a gray smear, and there was, again, the muttering of the earth, then silence. He trembled for Telien; thought resolutely of what must be done, created a prayer for Telien that must be heard by something; somewhere there was that that could heed him, though it was not the Luff'Eresi. Then he looked down across the hills toward Burgdeeth and thought of the slave prison there and thought of facing Venniver, and his mind churned with apprehension. His memory of the slave cell, memory of Venniver's sadistic cruelty, of Venniver's whip across men's backs, was not pleasant.

At last he shrugged as if to shake off demons, squared his shoulders, and began to make his way over the hills toward Burgdeeth.

The hill grass was dry and crunched under his boots. Hares leaped away. There were no trees. Occasional misshapen boulders, black and twisting, rose against the setting sun. Tangles of sablevine lay here and there, turning red to mark the dying summer. There was no sunset, the sky was strangely green as he stood on the last hill looking down on Burgdeeth. He buried the wolf bell there, deep among rocks, and covered it with earth. To become Venniver's captive carrying the wolf bell would be to incite rage unimaginable from Burgdeeth's dark leader.

Directly below him were some uncultivated fields, beyond them tall stands of whitebarley nearly ready for harvest, and beyond these the housegardens, running on to the back of the town. The town itself was three times as big as when Ram had left it, looked more permanent, with cobbled streets and all the stone buildings completed, where before many had risen roofless and empty above mud streets. The new temple was shockingly beautiful, all of white stone. Behind it, the Landmaster's Set looked almost finished, with turrets and sloping roofs that hinted of rare luxury within. There was open ground before it, perhaps a parade ground, with some smaller buildings, then a high wall around three sides and partially finished on the fourth where it would join the temple. All this stood upon what had been bare, rough land when Ram last saw Burgdeeth. The great pit had been filled in and gardens planted across it. And there, between temple and town, the town square was completed and the statue in its center even more awesome than Ram remembered: so tall, the falling sun striking behind it edging the god's wings with light. The memory of the long years Jerthon had spent molding each piece tightened Ram's throat. He thought of the secret tunnel beneath the statue, and wondered if he would need it in some wild escape from Venniver's execution fire—but the Luff'Eresi would come; he had only to get himself captured.

He saw that the slave cell was gone, though the guard tower still stood. There was a garden beside it now as if someone lived there. With no slave cell, what did Venniver do with his captives? Or were captives not kept alive long enough to house in any cell? Did Venniver not keep slaves any more?

Ram saw that women and girls were working the gardens. Perhaps with enough women to do the heavy garden work, and with the building of the town nearly complete, Venniver had no need of slaves. And perhaps, after Jerthon's rising against him and almost taking the town, he felt that the keeping of slaves was too risky.

Ram made his way across the fallow fields and through the stands of whitebarley, onto a path between the gardens.

At once a woman, kneeling and half-hidden in the mawzee, looked up, saw his red hair and rose up frightened to run silently toward the Hall. Another woman slipped away and disappeared around the end of the Hall. "*A Seer! A Seer comes!*"

He looked across the gardens to the doorway of the storeroom where he and Tayba had lived those dark, unsettling months, and a sharp picture came to him of the cluttered room, of his cot wedged between thresher and barrels, of the low rafters hung with cobwebs and the smell of grain; then he saw the room washed with dark and confusion, disappearing into evil blackness as the Seer Har-Thass took his mind away, tortured his mind, tortured his very soul until he lay feverish and near to dying, not knowing where he was or what he was.

Guards were coming on the double around both ends of the Hall. Ram stood facing them, wanting to run, held himself still with great effort.

They were robed in red. He supposed they called themselves deacons now, according to Venniver's grand plan. They surrounded him. One prodded him, one lunged to take his sword and Ram hit him, fought them then because not to fight would seem suspicious, because he could not help himself, kicked one captor in the groin sending him reeling, fought the dozen guards with mounting fury until they had pinned him at last.

They bound his arms and began to prod him toward the hall. He went slowly and sullenly, resisting them at every step, would not speak, would not answer their questions. They forced him past the hall toward Burgdeeth's main street, and there they made a great show of his capture, roaring commands so all along the street heads popped out of windows, folk ran out to watch. A man hauling barrels pulled up his donkey to stare; two women with milk cans set down their burdens to watch Ram forced along the cobbled street toward the square. He could smell hot wax, smell cess and the sour stench of ale brewing. Men and women crowded the street now, their hands stained from their work, their faces flushed with sudden excitement and with the self-rightousness that lay thinly concealing their blood-lust. He could see the hunger in their faces for the death of the Seer come so boldly into Burgdeeth, could see their growing anticipation of the exalted, killing fire so soon to burn in temple. A handful of children stared after him, their faces white with fear, then turned and ran. Ram was forced toward the square. Behind him the mountains rumbled faintly like a great animal yawning. Men turned, stared at the mountain, then stared back at Ram.

And then beyond the heads of the crowd he saw Venniver riding out from the Set and went weak with sudden fear; the sight of Venniver, the memories he stirred, sickened Ram. Broad of shoulder, black-bearded, his blue eyes cold as ice, he rode slowly toward the square where Ram stood, and Ram was a child again, defiant and afraid. Would Venniver recognize him? But perhaps not, for Ram's hair had been dyed black then. The mountain rumbled again. Venniver glanced toward it, then returned his gaze to Ram. Behind him, smoke hung in the sky above the mountains. He jerked his horse up with a hard hand so the animal began to fidget and would not settle. Venniver sat staring down at Ram like a hunting animal regarding cornered prey.

Whether he recognized Ram or not, it was clear that Venniver intended that this Seer should die—here in Burgdeeth, very soon, and with impressive ceremony.

On the mountains, Telien listened with growing apprehension to the rumbling earth, felt its quaking with an increasing sense of confusion, felt as if the mountains themselves might come tumbling down on her. The air was hot and close, smelled of sulphur. She could not put from her mind the Herebian tales of people running before flowing lakes of fire, burned to death as they fled.

Below in the meadow, the mare moved restlessly, looking often toward the mountains. The red stallion had disappeared. Telien could not believe he had deserted them. The mare gazed at the sky and spread her poor naked wings in a gesture that tore at Telien.

Then suddenly a shadow dropped over Telien. The stallion was descending, plummeting down to nudge the mare wildly, as if he would carry her aloft. He was irritable, seemed strung tight with agitation, nosed at Meheegan with terrible, loving urgency, wanted her to move out—but where could she go? Telien snatched up her bit of food, her blanket, and when she turned she saw the sky behind her grown dark with smoke. By the time she reached the valley floor she was drenched with sweat. Her horse was gone, had broken his reins. She hoped he would find safety.

The stallion greeted her with his head against her shoulder, then nudged her too, began to force both her and the mare toward the opposite rim of the valley. Surely the mare was aware of what he wanted, but seemed too frightened to obey, terrified of her helpless crippled entrapment upon the earth.

The three of them climbed until darkness overtook them, the darkness of night or the darkness of smoke filling the sky, it was hard to say which. They went along a ridge as the moons rose, dull smears obscured by smoke and giving little light. The stallion forced Meheegan on up the stony crest as the earth trembled again and again. He seemed to be heading directly into the face of the fires. Now and then he would rise into the smoke-filled sky, and each time return to change direction, to hurry them faster up the rising ridge; to reassure the stumbling mare, so heavy and clumsy with her unborn foal. Once Meheegan laid her head against Telien's shoulder, so tired, so driven and afraid.

As the ridge rose more steeply to join the mountain, the mare climbed by balancing with her poor naked wings. Telien pulled herself up by clutching at boulders, could not believe the mare *could* climb as she was doing up the rocky incline. The stallion's wings, as he balanced, spread over them as if to shelter them from the violent sky. The earth rocked harder, its voice swept them with fear. Then the earth shook like an animal, and Telien stumbled, lost her hold; the mountain tilted, and she was thrown against a boulder, clutched at it, was torn from it—she was falling.

She fell twisting down the cliff, grabbing at dirt, and could not stop herself, heard the mare scream as the whole world rocked and spun.

When at last the ground was still, Telien could not rise. She lay in the near dark, dizzy and confused. She could see the rocky slope down which she had fallen. She heard the mare groan close by. Finally she raised herself, began to crawl until she found Meheegan's warm bulk sprawled above her up the slope, went sick at the thought of broken legs; how could the mare fall so far and not break every bone? The stallion nickered, a darker shape against the smoke-filled sky, nosing at Meheegan, caressing and reassuring her, trying to make her rise.

At last Meheegan threw up her head and began to struggle to get up. Telien forgot her own pain and confusion as she watched Meheegan's painful effort. She could not believe it when the mare stood on all four legs.

Once the stallion had Meheegan up, he began to nose at Telien—though he drew back and snorted when his muzzle touched her forehead. She touched her head and felt blood.

She rose at last, very dizzy, leaned against the stallion and heard him nicker to the mare. He wanted to climb again, to be away. How could they climb again that rocky cliff? It was not possible. She was too dizzy to climb anywhere, too sick to climb.

But they did climb. With terrible effort, Telien and the mare climbed the dark, rocky incline with the stallion pushing constantly at them, nearly dragging Telien sometimes as she clung to him, forcing the mare, giving all his weight to brace her as she struggled upward, his wings supporting and buoying them, keeping them from reeling backward into the ravine. At last, at long last, they stood high atop a plateau on the mountain. Below them, red streaks broke the night where rivers of fire were flowing out.

Telien did not see the wolves above them in the darkness—wolves urging the stallion on—did not see the great dark wolf grin and his mate Rhymannie bow low as the three finally topped the slope. She did not see wolves swing away on noiseless feet to lead the red stallion ever upward between the fires of the mountains.

RAM STARED at Venniver's cold blue eyes and without warning the power returned to him, flooding him so he was suddenly and utterly aware of Venniver's mind. How could this happen so abruptly? Were the powers of the dark drawn away in some effort that took all the force they had? Or were the Luff'Eresi doing this for him, using their own great powers to give him this clear vision of Venniver? To open Venniver's mind to examination was not an easy task. Ram had never—when he had lived in Burgdeeth, when his powers had been full on him—been able to touch Venniver's mind like this; for Venniver had the rare skill of mind-blocking without ever knowing he did so: latent Seer's blood, of no use except for this. Now

Ram touched Venniver's greed for power, felt with all his being Venniver's hunger to enslave, saw the intricate gilded web of religion Venniver had laid like a trap over the minds he ruled; saw Venniver's fears as well, his awesome terror of Seers and his lusting hunger for their death. Venniver meant to call the service at once, to use the growing fury of the mountains to dramatize this sacrifice before his humble sheep. Ram grinned wryly. The dark leader's sense of drama was very fine. Ram contained his rising terror with effort, tried in desperation to speak in silence with the Luff'Eresi, prayed to them without calling it prayer. Prayed to whatever might be out there to hear him.

He was led directly beneath the winged statue and made to kneel. Ironic, this statue he had seen a-building, this statue that hid its own secret. The sky was dark with smoke, and with coming night. The wind smelled of burning and of sulphur. You're not going to die, Ramad my boy! Stop your quaking! He stared up at the statue and thought of Jerthon building it slowly piece by piece, of the slaves digging the tunnel beneath it slowly, every shovelful a triumph over Venniver. He was kneeling only inches from the tunnel's hidden door. Could he slip down there under cover of darkness?

Of course he could, with six deacons and the entire populace of Burgdeeth crowding around him! And even if he did escape, what of his careful plan to save the Children of Burgdeeth? He clung to his faith in the Luff'Eresi as Venniver shouted for firewood and coal to be brought at once to the temple.

Skeelie slept sprawled out across her bed every which way, woke suddenly, sat up, saw that the moons outside the stone portal had risen but hung muted as if they were covered by gray gauze. She heard the distant rumbling then and felt sudden, sharp fear. And she Saw, in a clear vision, torches flaring and Ram forced through Burgdeeth's square, and she knew he was meant to die. Her voice caught, was half scream *"Ram! Ramad!" Why was he in Burgdeeth, why had he gone to Burgdeeth?* She rose to stare blindly out at the sea trying to bring a force that would help him, trying to turn away his captors, to force her power upon them . . .

Uselessly. Uselessly.

Had the gods refused him, had he gone to Burgdeeth then, alone, with some wild plan? The vision ceased abruptly as Ram was forced up the steps of the temple. She stared blindly at the sea, then stirred, struck flint, and ran barefoot down the corridor to Tayba's room.

The door was open. Tayba was pacing, her dark hair loose, her slim hands holding the runestone. The moonlight caught at it as she turned; Jerthon stood in shadow with Drudd and Pol. All of them had seen the vision. Tayba looked up at Skeelie, said softly, "Ram has spoken with the gods." She shuddered, continued.

"The gods would have him do this, Skeelie. He is . . . Ram is a decoy. He . . . They will rescue him, they will not let him die. Or so—so Ram believes." She turned suddenly to Jerthon. "*Why* did the vision come just now, so clear? What made the dark pull away? Is Ram—is Ram in such danger that in spite of the dark, the very force of his fear makes us able to See? Is he . . . ?"

Jerthon shook his head, his green eyes dark in the dulled moonlight; far off the mountains rumbled. "The earth speaks, Tayba, listen to it. The fires of the mountains speak." How strange his voice was. "Maybe that is what gives us this sudden power. If . . ." He looked deeply at Tayba, his excitement leaping between them. "If the fires of the mountain can part the dark—can we use that force to help Ram?

"We—we must try. We . . ."

He seemed very remote for a moment. "I think that the power in the mountains is a force not of good or of evil. A force unknowing and uncaring of both. Somehow—perhaps by our constant vigilance, by our very concern for Ram, perhaps by Ram's fear itself, we have drawn that power to the side of good. Now—yes, now we must use it for Ram."

They stood in silence reaching with their minds and with the power of the stone, the five of them willing Ram's safety. Skeelie clung with her very soul to that power of the mountain, bent her will stubbornly and humbly to draw upon that power, forced her own meager strength to battle for Ram's life harder than ever she had as a child, when she had fought so desperately to keep the dark back.

Chapter Eight

IN THE CASTLE of Hape, the battle to control the raw power of the mountains stilled the dark Seers so they seemed as stone. The Hape itself was not visible, but its force was linked with the Seers; and even so the dark powers faltered. For now the Seers of Carriol held power. And on the mountains, fire spewed like blood, fiery rivers oozing down along the valleys burning scrub so grass could spring anew: fires renewing by killing; and the night sky was heavy with smoke as flame burst from far peaks.

In Burgdeeth, while the mountains rumbled with mute voices, Ram was forced up the temple steps—thinking of Telien, thinking now only of Telien somewhere among those fires. And inside the temple the silent citizens knelt with bowed heads and righteous thoughts, anticipating the ritual of the Seer's death by fire, so anticipating their own sacred redemption.

Ram had been stripped naked and his hands and legs bound with leather thongs. He was led hobbling to the altar, the leather biting into his ankles, and there he was forced to kneel. His fear of death rose again in spite of his control, as Venniver stood above him, blank of expression, robed in ceremonial white. On the dais behind the red-robed deacons, wood and charcoal had been laid against the tall iron stake. Venniver's voice rose to echo in the domed temple. "The gods speak!"

The people answered as one, "The gods speak."

"The gods command the Seer's death!"

"They command *death!*"

"Evil must be destroyed by fire, by the cleansing fire!"

"The fire! The sacred fire!"

Ram was chilled, but sweating. Venniver's voice rang like thunder through the temple. "Those with the curse of Ynell, those with the curse of Seeing, are as filth upon the land!"

"The fire! The sacred fire!"

Two deacons pulled Ram upright, forced him up the steps to the iron stake. He stared at the oil-soaked wood around his feet with a feeling of terror he could not quell, felt the bonds tighten as he was bound to the stake. He prayed then, in cold silence. The mountains rumbled. Venniver glanced up, seemed to take this as an omen to his righteousness. The kneeling people sighed faintly. Ram knew terror, knew it was too late to fight back now, he had left it too long.

"They who defy the powers of the gods shall be consumed in fire!"

"The fire! The sacred fire . . ."

"Must die! Die by fire! The Seer must die by fire!"

"Die by fire!" Their voices rose, and they began to stir.

Venniver held up his hands. Their voices stilled as one. He knelt dramatically before the funeral pyre, and the sheep sighed. Venniver seemed then to be praying, made long dramatic ritual all in silence, lighting of candles along the altar as the deacons chanted in deep, reverent voices. Ram stood watching with growing horror his own funeral, sweating, his body numbed by the tightly cutting bonds.

Venniver rose at last, made signs of obeisance before

the raised altar, turned to face the temple.

Strung by fear, trying to keep himself from screaming out, Ram tried to touch Venniver's thoughts and could not. He tried to hold steady to the Luff'Eresi's promise and was overwhelmed by terror as Venniver took up a taper, struck flint so it flared and, smiling, thrust the flaming taper to the pyre. Flame leaped, caught, flared up Ram's bare legs. He fought in terror, unable to control himself.

But the flame died. Died as if it had been snuffed. The sheep stared and sucked in their breath.

Venniver lit the pyre again. Again the flame leaped, again died. The taper in his hand died to blackness, and suddenly the temple door flew open. A woman screamed, men rose from their benches to stare, light poured into the temple brighter than moonlight and icy cold: blinding light, fracturing, dancing light; and from the light a voice boomed.

"*Unbind the Seer! You tamper with our property, pig of Burgdeeth! Unbind the Seer that belongs to us!*"

Venniver stood staring, seemed afraid—yet squared his shoulders in defiance. He seemed about to speak when suddenly his body twisted until he knelt, screaming out in pain.

"*Free the Seer!*"

Venniver scowled. He tried to rise and could not.

"*Free the Seer, pig of Burgdeeth!*"

At last, in obvious pain, Venniver nodded to a deacon, and Ram felt his bonds loosed from behind, felt the brush of a deacon's robe.

"*Bring the Seer here!*"

Venniver stared at the cold light, again was twisted so he knelt; again nodded to a deacon.

Two deacons came forward, took Ram's arms, and he was led down the steps of the altar, past the sheep, and stood at last in the door of the temple facing the shattering radiance of a dozen winged gods towering over him, their horselike bodies and human torsos ever-changing in the shifting light—light that seemed a part of them. Ram went down to them, walked among them to the square with head bowed and eyes lowered as if he were their prisoner; felt their amusement and returned it with his own, wanted to shout with pleasure and release. He turned at last to see Venniver and his deacons forced out of the temple as if they were pulled by invisible lines. They tried to turn away but could not get free, and their faces were frozen in terror.

The leaders of Burgdeeth were forced toward the square and there made to kneel before the winged statue of gods. The Luff'Eresi towered around the statue, so brilliant one could hardly look, cast their light across the bronze figures so they, too, seemed alive.

The sky in the east was a dull red as the Luff'Eresi spoke again. "*Call out your people, Venniver of Burgdeeth.*"

The people of Burgdeeth came hesitantly to the square, mobbed together in fear just as fearful sheep would mob, stood before the Luff'Eresi at last, and then knelt of one accord; and they could not look up at that brilliance, none had the courage to look up though the brilliance touched them like a benevolence.

"*Unbind the Seer's hands! We have no need to bind our prisoners. Do you expect us to take him like a sack of meal! This is our prisoner you have so brazenly played with!*"

Ram was unbound. Stood naked and free and cared not for his nakedness, felt only triumph as he saw Venniver cower before the Luff'Eresi.

"*Listen well, Venniver of Burgdeeth! We tend our own sacrifices. That is* our *privilege.* We *deal with the Seers, not you. If you claim another Seer—man, child or woman—you will die. Die wishing you had never been born!*

"*Do you hear us well?*"

"I—hear you well." Venniver glanced up sideways at the gods, then looked down again; his great breadth and height, the bulk of the man, which always made others look puny, had gone. He seemed a small, shrinking figure now before these magnificent beings. For an instant, the thunder of the mountains drowned all else. Fire leaped skyward in the east, and at that sign the men of Burgdeeth moaned as if all their pent-up terror was suddenly freed into sound. They knelt moaning before the gods; and Venniver's deacons knelt; and the Luff'Eresi thundered, *"From now hence for all time you will bring the Seers to us! Do you understand, pig of Burgdeeth?"*

"I understand."

"I understand, master!"

"I understand, master."

Among the kneeling crowd, some of Venniver's soldiers had begun to rise now, and to slip fearfully away, seeking their horses, seeking escape. The Luff'Eresi ignored them.

*"Open your mind, Venniver of Burgdeeth, and we will mark the path you will take to bring the prisoners to us! For you will bring them—*all *of them—to the death stone outside of Eresu. There* we *will deal with them. One transgression, Venniver of Burgdeeth, one omission, and your own death will be so long and painful an experience that you will beg to die!*

"And think not," cried the Luff'Eresi as one, *"that we will not know what you do here. We see your petty intrigues, human! We see your insignificant thoughts!*

"You will not defy us again, pig of Burgdeeth!"

Ram felt a stir of air, looked up to see the silver stallion plummeting down out of the sky, heard the indrawn breath of men as they dared to look up, in spite of the gods' radiance, to see the winged stallion descend. The stallion came at once to Ram, and he swung himself up between the great wings, stared down at Venniver's white face, at the awe-struck sheep, and tried to look as submissive and captive as possible, though his spirit was soaring with this taste of triumph and freedom. As the stallion whirled, he saw a handful of men riding hard away from Burgdeeth, saw them felled suddenly. They lay unmoving as their riderless horses fled. And then suddenly the silver stallion leaped skyward and Ram was lifted, was windborne on the night sky between the stallion's sweeping wings, surrounded by light and by the wild exalted laughter of the Luff'Eresi, filling Ram's mind with joy.

In the ruins, Jerthon lifted his head from deepest concentration. Ram was safe, Ram had lifted free of Burgdeeth. He saw tears in Tayba's eyes. Skeelie was leaning, pale with her effort, against the sill of the portal. She turned from him abruptly, swung out of the room, was gone. Jerthon could sense her striding along the corridor toward the Citadel. She would kneel there alone, would pray, would thank whatever there was to thank that Ramad was safe.

Tayba's voice was no more than a whisper, so shaken was she with her effort, with the fear that had gripped her. With the wonder of that moment when the gods had spoken. For they had all Seen the gods clearly, Seen Venniver quail before the Luff'Eresi. The five of them had stared at each other in wild exaltation. "Was it . . ." Tayba whispered now. "*Is* it the power of the gods that we feel, Jerthon? Or the power of the mountains, as you said?"

"I don't know. Perhaps—perhaps both." He studied her quietly. "But this . . . this I know. That power—and I feel it still, do you not?" She nodded. "That power, whatever it is . . ." He did not need to finish, they all knew, they lifted their faces in sudden eagerness at his thoughts: Yes! This power must not be wasted! This power must be used, and now. Used while it flowed strong, while they felt it buoying them, urging them on. "We will arm at once," Jerthon said softly. "Ready supplies, men, horses. We will ride for Pelli in a day's time. Now is the moment to destroy the Pellian Seers if ever we are to do it!"

They stared at him, lifted and renewed. To attack Pelli, to attack the dark Seers and the Hape. Yes! As one, Tayba and Drudd and Pol turned, preparing to depart, to give orders for supplies, for preparations. Jerthon stopped them with a quiet thought. They stood watching him, waiting. "There—there is enough power, if it holds, to block our thoughts from Skeelie. She—she will be wanting badly to ride out before dawn. A vision touches me . . ." He looked at them, questioning. The others felt out. Tayba nodded, then Drudd and Pol. "Yes," Jerthon said. "Skeelie will touch that vision, she will soon know that Ram will come to Blackcob—come in some need. She—would be with him then. I think—I think she should go unknowing." Again there were nods of agreement. If Skeelie knew about the attack on Pelli, Ram would know soon; she could not keep such a thing from Ram's mind as long as this sudden power surrounded them. *They* could keep it from Ram, perhaps, but Skeelie never could. Yes, the next moments, the next day, would be a time that might never come again for Ram. The next hours might never be remade, would be gone all too soon.

"Let them be," Drudd said. "Let the young ones be. They will help us in battle in their own time."

They nodded again, turned, went out of the chamber to prepare for war.

Telien had slept heavily, as if she were drugged, woke with a throbbing pain in her head and did not know where she was. She tried to understand why the darkness was so red. Why was her room so hot? She smelled smoke. She stared at the walls and saw that this was not her room, not any ordinary room, but a rough cave, and dark. The red light outside was . . . She rose on her elbow to stare. Was—*fire! Fire!* In a panic she tried to rise and was dizzy, sank down to the stone shelf again, trembling and sick and confused, had to get out, could feel the heat now, terrifying her.

Finally she could sit up, was calmer, saw there was no flame near, only the red sky through the cave's high opening, remembered the mountains. But how did she get here? She rose, stumbling, knelt beside Meheegan who only raised her head, moaned low. She made her way up to the cave's mouth. Her heart was pounding. She stood at the cave's mouth, facing the flaming mountains.

And she saw that the red light was from reflection in the sky, that fire flared on peaks below and around her, but there was no fire here on this mountain—though below her the ridges shone red where a fiery river ran down, flaring suddenly as it struck a huge tree.

Behind her, Meheegan stirred with a moaning sigh. The smoke made Telien's eyes water. The mountain rumbled faintly, then the only sound was the hiss of cooling steam and the hush-hush of slow-burning foliage far below. Were the flames dying, was the mountain's tantrum subsiding? She remembered it all now—their journey up the mountain—but did not remember how she had come to this cave, remembered very little after she had fallen. Her head hurt so. She stared out at the red, angry turmoil of the mountains, sweating, her face prickly. After some moments of the unbearable heat, she made her way down again to the cooler interior, pausing once with the sick dizziness of nausea, which finally passed. She had a vague memory of climbing up rock. Had they climbed here, she and Meheegan? But they must have. She could remember the red stallion forcing and pushing at her.

Below her the mare had risen and begun to move

restlessly back and forth. Telien saw the stallion then, at the far side of the cave, lying out full length, his wings folded around him. What was the matter with him? Was he . . . ? He raised his head and nickered to reassure her, and she let out her breath in relief.

Telien stood watching Meheegan pace, driven by the pain of labor. The stallion rose at last and came to push tenderly at Meheegan as, again, nausea swept Telien. She knelt, weak and miserable, and was sick.

She did not see the wolves watching from the deep shadows of the cave, waiting in silence for the mare's extravagant event. But she felt a calmness suddenly, and a strengthening. She rose and went to touch the mare, to try to comfort her and steady her against the pain. The mare groaned and tightened herself, crouching, straining.

The pains and constrictions came sharper, closer. Then, as the first touch of morning began to wash the sky, so drifts of ash could be seen on the hot wind, the foal began to come slipping out, a silvery sack. There was blood. The mare groaned. Telien knelt, fighting the sickness and nausea, trying to help. Her hands shook.

It was then that the wolves crept out, silent and huge and gentle. The silver-encased foal sought strongly to tear itself away from the last vestige of dark, warm safety, to leave the womb in a madness of life-lust, in a questing after a mystery it did not understand, yet sought with all its strength. The mare screamed. The foal slipped free. At once a pale wolf came forward and tore the sack open, and then Meheegan turned and began to lick the new young stallion that unfolded from its fetal shape. Telien watched, half-drugged with dizziness and pain, but missing none of the wonder; and then she went limp, sprawled across the cave, her head wound bleeding harder.

The five wolves stood over her. One licked away the blood. The dark dog wolf put his face close to hers and seemed reassured by her faint but steady breathing. They watched the foal begin to wriggle, trying almost at once to loose those tight-folded stubs of wings. The wolves watched as it tried to rise on long, rubbery legs; and they watched Telien wake and saw her fear of them.

She stared up at wolves all around her, huge and shaggy and rank-smelling, and fear cut through her, sharp and cold. The largest, a dark, broad dog wolf, approached her. His head was immense, his eyes stared unblinking.

But his expression was not an animal expression, was so very human. She looked up at him partly in fear and partly with rising wonder; and in excited desperation she thought Ram's name, Ramad of wolves. "Ramad," she croaked, and put out her hand. Were these wolves Ram's brothers? She was so dizzy, and still very much afraid in spite of her rising excitement. Animals hated fear. The big dog wolf came close to her. She knew, somehow, that she was expected to touch him.

She reached. Her hand trembled. His teeth gleamed in a—was it a smile? He grinned widely, she could see the dark roof of his mouth. When she touched his face at last, the little hairs along his muzzle were soft as velvet. He looked down at her not as a wolf would look, and she repeated, "Ramad," gone in terror. Gone in wonder.

The wolf licked her hand and lay his head on her shoulder, and his gentleness wiped away her fear. How could she have feared him? She looked across at Meheegan and Rougier and realized that the mare and stallion had never been afraid; they stood among the wolves in perfect friendship.

In the dim cave the red stallion and the five great wolves, the exhausted mare, and Telien stood watching—all alike in their wonder—as the new foal sought to rise and spread his wings. A colt red as his sire, born among the flames of the mountains. And Telien thought, Ram will love him. Then tears for Ram came suddenly and painfully, and she crouched against the shaggy dog wolf clutching his coat and weeping for Ram, washed with a sense of Ram's danger, wanting Ram and so afraid for him.

But then all at once, without Seer's skill, her mind lay open. The dark wolf spoke in her mind, and she saw Ram bound to the stake, saw fire blaze around his naked legs. She knew this was a vision of something past. She heard a faint chanting, *the fire, the sacred fire,* and then she saw the glancing shattering brightness of the Luff'Eresi descending upon Burgdeeth and saw the dark Burgdeeth leader—black of beard, broad of shoulder—quail before the gods. And she saw Ram loosed from his bonds. She saw Ram carried aloft on the back of the silver stallion amidst the bright dazzle of the gods and knew that he was safe.

RAM RODE BETWEEN the stallion's wings, oblivious to the fury of the Pellian leaders at his escape. Oblivious to their dark push to touch his mind. So numbed by exhaustion was he that only an echo remained in his mind of the Luff'Eresi's voices, swelling with laughter and thundering victory. They had risen with him above Burgdeeth, then, very high above the hills, their light had shattered all around him and they had vanished. Simply vanished; the night sky suddenly empty except for the smoke-dulled light of Ere's moons.

The victory in Burgdeeth had been fine. Riding now free in the night, the wind chilling his naked body, Ram grinned at the memory of Venniver's face, twisted with rage and fear, with submission.

Below, flames licked down to touch hills and meadows, but the mountains themselves seemed to have calmed. He could see no flame there now. Dalwyn dropped his silver wings in a glide and brought Ram down to the hill where the wolf bell lay buried. Ram retrieved it, searching in darkness, then crouching naked among stone, digging. Then they leaped skyward again, the stallion keeping well south of the fires. They flew low over hills where thin fingers of lava crept down in the deepest creases. Ram could see, at some distance, a few dim lights burning where Kubal lay; and the stallion had begun to drop toward that place. Ram felt the horse's quick humor and agreed he needed clothes.

Where one guard stood with his back to them, the stallion came noiselessly down out of the sky to land without a stir of air.

Ram sized up the man's height and width of shoulder. Yes, these clothes would do fine. His pulse quickened. He poised ready, moved silently.

Ram took the guard's clothes and left him naked and unconscious in a tangle of sablevine; fingered the weapons and was glad he had left a few in Kubal. Now, perhaps, the Kubalese would learn to hunt with clubs. When he turned to the silver stallion, he stood with his hand on the great horse's neck, tried to reach out to Telien, to sense her somewhere in those mountains, and could not.

"Can you find her, Dalwyn? If she lives among those fires, can you find her? Can you sense the red stallion and his mare?"

Dalwyn turned to stare toward the dark mountains. He would try. His every nerve went taut, trying to sense Rougier and Meheegan, to sense the invisible. They would go among the mountains. They would try.

Ram knelt beside a spring and washed and drank. He smelled the stink of the borrowed clothes, made a face, wished he had found a cleaner guard.

Dalwyn was sloshing and drinking, enjoying the water thoroughly. Ram's wonder was never diminished that even this horse-like action was as a man would do, that every action of the horses of Eresu was a sentient, balanced action, unhorse-like in the extreme. The stallion turned to him at last; Ram swung himself up, and they leaped skyward so fast he was almost unseated, were heading at once into deep smoke and heat.

On the land beneath them, smoking lava lay cooling, little flames licking out where grass and bushes still burned. As they rose toward the higher peaks, Ram prayed for Telien. And prayed that if she had died, it was quickly and without pain.

To think of her dead was unbearable; Telien could not be dead. He would know in the same way he had known, when first he saw her, that they were linked in a way he might never understand. Telien had never really left him since that moment on Tala-charen. All the women he had known since had been judged against her. Skeelie had been judged against her, good, faithful Skeelie whom he otherwise might have loved; Skeelie, who was his sister, his mother, his friend, but never anything more—because of Telien.

It was dawn on the road between the ruins and Blackcob. Skeelie and the old Seer, Berd, and a few soldiers rode hunched over, sleepy, sated with a huge breakfast. They had left in darkness, the pack horses only black lumps at the ends of their lead ropes; desperate to get to Blackcob because they knew there would be a need there. They rode now along the edge of the dark sea, the breakers making a pattern of white movement against darkness. The sea's pounding seemed not a part of that pattern, seemed a delayed echo from the recent wild thunder of the mountains.

What they would find in Blackcob was largely unclear. They had watched all night the fiery sky, heard the rattling cries of the mountains. But only glimpses had come to them of the seething land itself. Skeelie had held for one brief instant a clear vision of Ram leaping skyward from Burgdeeth amidst the fiery sky, had known with elation Ram's victory and the victory of the gods of Eresu—Carriol's victory over Venniver's sadism. She stared ahead in the direction of Blackcob, buoyed by this victory against the pain that awaited her there. She could not extricate herself from the blackness into which she had been driven when first she heard, from the refugees coming out of Blackcob, that Ram had found Telien. She had turned away, fists clenched when they spoke of the two of them whispering together their good-bys.

Ram would be coming to Blackcob, she knew that clearly. How or why, she did not know. But she must see him once more. See for herself that he was lost to her. She pulled her cape around her, found she was hugging herself in a desolate passion of loneliness.

Yet still hope rose in spite of logic, and she rode for Blackcob with some wild unexamined notion that maybe . . . maybe . . .

She knew Ram would ride for Blackcob strung tight with some urgent need, come there in wild desperation. And when she was honest with herself, she had to wonder: Did she ride for Blackcob with the hope that Ram would come there in grief, having lost Telien to the holocaust of the mountains? Yes, if she were honest, she knew she wished Telien dead. Wished her gone, and wished to console Ram in his sorrow.

Yet Telien's death would make no difference; Ram would love Telien, not until she died, but until he died.

Tears touched her cheeks. No matter the pain of her jealousy, she wanted no pain for Ram. No matter her own sorrow, underneath her hatred she wanted Telien to live—for Ram. For Ram to be happy. Wanting that, Skeelie was more miserable than ever.

She had insisted on going, had stared into Jerthon's eyes with fine defiance and seen his hurt for her, had sworn at him for a fool. "I don't go because of Ram! I go because they will need me. If there are wounded, burned from the fire . . ."

"You go because Ram will come there, Skeelie girl. And you . . ." He had left the rest unsaid. Great fires of Urdd! Sometimes she wished they were none of them Seers and could never, never See one into the mind of another!

THE STALLION CHANGED DIRECTION SUDDENLY, seeking over the fiery land, winged over and down into a blast of hot wind then through a narrow valley, rock walls rising beside them. Ram clung, saw not the walls or the smokey sky, Saw a clear vision suddenly of Telien kneeling, white and sick, beside the newborn foal. He heard Telien's thoughts as if they were his own: was death the same as birth? Was death, too, a wild struggling after a mystery we cannot know, can only sense? He shouted into the hot wind, "Don't speak of death! Don't think of death!" And only the stallion heard him.

He felt the stallion sweep suddenly in a different direction, seeking again, disoriented and unable to touch the others with his thoughts. The great horse's direction was confused and uncertain. They soared low between mountains where smoke still rose sullenly, dropped down across a valley that steamed from the cooling lava. Everywhere there was lava going gray, burned brush and trees. The sweating stallion moved with the same uncertainty that a crippled bat might move, sensing his direction then foiled of it suddenly, blinded again so his course changed, changed again. Dalwyn grew weary, his wings heavy; the hot air did not hold him well. He came down at last to rest.

It was well after midday. Ram dismounted beside a

stream bed dried up, the land above it charred. Between ancient boulders he found a protected place where the heat had not come so fiercely and dug with his knife until at last he uncovered a bit of dampness. They waited for an interminable time until the water had oozed up to make a small pool from which Dalwyn could drink. Ram said, "You cannot hold the sense of the red stallion, Dalwyn. Will we ever find them?"

Dalwyn lifted his head. He did not know. Rougier would come into his mind then fade at once, and Dalwyn's idea of the direction would twist and become confused. He was as the hunting birds of old Opensa that were whirled around in baskets until they had no notion of which way were their eyries, and so returned to their masters at last in confused submission.

So were the dark Seers confusing Dalwyn now.

"But why? Such a little thing as finding Telien . . ." Ram stared at the stallion with rising anger. "Why should BroogArl care if . . ." Then he stiffened. *Why should BroogArl care?* And why should he *not* care? It was Telien—*Telien* who would bring another stone into Ere!

Of course BroogArl wanted her lost. Lost to Ram and to Ere, forever. Ram laid a hand on Dalwyn's withers, touched his sweating sides. "We *must* find her, and soon." He took off his jerkin and began to rub the stallion down, wiping away sweat, smoothing his coat. When water had seeped again into the cupped sand, Dalwyn drank a second time, then they were off, Ram forcing his powers now against BroogArl, against the Hape, in an aching effort to stay the dark while Dalwyn circled, sought out Rougier, and swept off in a direction from which they had recently come. The air was smokey, drifting with ash, so hot in some places, that their vision was blurred. Ram held with great effort against the dark, felt the strength of the wolf bell sustaining him, held so until at last Dalwyn swept down suddenly and surely to the mouth of a cave high in a dark peak, and Ram knew she was there, could sense her there.

Dalwyn came down fast to the lip of the cave. Ram slid off and was inside running downward into the darkness. He startled the mare. The little foal jumped away from him in alarm. He laid a hand on the mare's cheek. He was sorry to have frightened her. But Telien—Telien was not there.

He searched the small cave for other openings. There was one; but he turned back to the entrance, the mare directed him back. Dalwyn called to him in silence.

Outside on the mountain, he followed the silver stallion up a thin thread of path that climbed steeply beside a steep drop. The heat was terrible here, rising from the burned hills. He found Telien at last, lying cold as death, inches from the drop. How could she be cold? The air was stifling. She was barely conscious, shivering, her skin like ice. He lifted her and held her, trying to warm her. She whispered so low he could barely hear her, "The ice—it's so slippery. I can't climb, I can't get to the grass. She is so hungry . . ."

Ice? The mountain was hot as Urdd. And yet her hands and face were freezing cold, her tunic cold and wet and, in the creases, stiff with ice crystals that melted at his touch. He stared at the swollen, blood-crusted wound on her forehead, and a memory of just such a wound made him feel the pain again. He knew at once the dizziness she felt, the nausea, guessed her confused state.

But why was she cold?

Her arms and legs, her face were scraped and dirty. Her legs were black with ash but smeared, too, with the melting ice. Beneath the grit her skin was pale. Her hair was tangled with twigs and dead sablevine and dulled with ashes. When he tried to smooth it, she sighed, reached to touch his hand, then dropped her own hand, palm up curving in innocence. But then she looked at him suddenly without recognition, fell into sleep again, frightening him anew.

He carried her down into the cave and laid her on a stone shelf, covered her with his dirty tunic. The cave was cooler, but still stifling. Telien shivered. He began to chafe her wrists, then at last he lay down over her, keeping his weight off but trying to warm her. She stirred a little then, opened her eyes. She was shivering uncontrollably. "The snow comes so hard. Will it never stop? There is ice . . . the path . . . I must not fall. Meheegan . . ."

"Telien! Telien!"

She had gone unconscious again. He gathered her close, trying to warm her, trying to understand what had happened. She shivered again. He must get her warm or she would die. He rose, stared around the cave. He had flint, but there was nothing here to burn. It was then he saw the wolves come around him suddenly out of the darkness. Fawdref nuzzled close to him in wild greeting, his great tail swinging an arc. Rhymannie stared up at him grinning with joy. They came at once onto the shelf with Telien and lay down all around her, covering her. They had dropped their kill at Ram's feet, three fat rock hare.

Ram could see little more of Telien now than her cheek and one strand of pale hair, so completely did the wolves cover her. Rhymannie began to lick her face. Ram took up the rock hares, carried them to the mouth of the cave and began to clean them. Telien would need food, something hot. But where in Urdd was he going to get fuel? Fawdref spoke in his mind then, showed Ram where there was grass on the mountain, and he understood that Telien had been trying to climb there to gather it for the mare.

He went up the narrow steep trail to gather the grasses dried brown by the heat and to gather some of the dried manure left by the winged ones. He returned to the cave, built a fire, and cut the rock hare into small portions to cook quickly. When the first pieces were done, he woke Telien. She ate slowly, watching Ram, uncertain still of her surroundings. She discovered the wolves clustered over and around her, was afraid, then lost her fear as suddenly and pulled Rhymannie's muzzle down to her in affection, sighing with the life-giving warmth. Ram had brought grass for the mare. She ate with the dispatch of one truly hungry, while her greedy young colt nursed, flapping his stubby wings with pleasure.

When Telien had eaten, her color was better, her eyes clearer. "It was so cold, Ram. Did the snow melt? It's warm now; how long has it been? When did you come here?" She stared up toward the cave opening, puzzled. "The mountains were white with it. And you—you haven't any tunic. You . . ."

"Hush." He knelt, laid a hand over her lips. "It's all right. I found you on the ledge, you were almost frozen. Where—it was hot, Telien. The air is like steam. Where . . . what happened to you?"

"I don't—I don't know. I was . . ." She tried to sit up, so Rhymannie's head was lifted on her shoulder. Ram helped her. The wolves stirred, resettled themselves around her. She stared across the dim cave at the mare, saw the foal. "I—I was going up to get grass for Meheegan, she . . . on the mountain. The wolves said . . ." She startled, looked at Ram with amazement. "They—the wolves spoke to me, Ram. Spoke in my mind . . ." Her eyes were filled with wonder. "How can that be? I—I am no Seer."

"Tell me what happened."

"They showed me—in my mind—where the grass was left untouched, and then they went to hunt. I went—I went up along the path and Rougier came flying up beside me in case, I—I was so dizzy. He stayed with me, and then suddenly he—he was gone and the path was all ice, the mountains white and—and then I don't remember—then you came, I guess." She reached to touch his face. "How—how did you find me here?"

"Dalwyn found you. I cannot, even with the wolf bell I could sense little." He knew he must go for food for her, for fuel. For water, grain for the mare. Telien needed herbs, bread, needed more than meat alone—and even rock hares must be hard to find after the fires, for surely game had perished. He laid a hand on the dark wolf's head. "Stay with her, Fawdref. Stay with her, hunt for her if I do—stay until I return." He tucked the tunic tighter around her, held her for a long moment, then rose and turned to the cave's entrance where Dalwyn waited, silhouetted like a dark statue against the ashen sky.

"Ram?"

He turned back. He thought he could not bear to leave her. They had been apart all their lives. Now, to part so soon was unthinkable. He saw her eyes, needing him, but knew that he must go. "The wolves—Fawdref and Rhymannie will care well for you. I will bring you food, cakes. What girl, Telien, what girl in Ere has such tender nurses?"

She smiled. "No girl. Not such nurses as these. Oh, Ram . . ." Her eyes grew large suddenly and darkened as if some foreshadowing had touched her. She glanced away, then back at him more lightly. "Don't be long, Ramad of wolves."

Fear twisted in his stomach as he mounted. He turned to look back at her, wanted to say, *Come with me, Telien.* But she was too weak. He watched Rhymannie reach to lick her face. He mounted the silver stallion and was gone into the sky.

Love's will cannot be drawn against the will of Time, but must swing with it. Love's fate cannot be shaped by the minds of those who love: except as they cleave to the infinity of power that carves out all life. Except as they cleave to the spirit that has birthed them.

There is no path through the fulcrum of Time, there is no promise that one will return, no promise that one will not die lost in Time and alone. There is no promise that what one seeks will be given.

And you who are Seer born, your mission is perilous. If you hold the power of the jade or hold a taint of that stone, those who are dark will lust for it, and follow.

And think not the gods to save you.

Think not the gods to meddle. To twist and warp your path through Time, and so destroy your freedom. You are thrown into Time alone, and so alone shall you travel. And if you come, one to another swept on the tides of Time, and if you cleave one to another, perhaps you cleave then to the power that carves out all life, to the spirit that has birthed you. And if you cleave so one to another, then shall you cleave to joy though Time itself spin you broken as flotsam upon its eternal shore.

Telien

Chapter Nine

Blackcob, scarred from the Kubalese raids, now stood sullen indeed with the ravages of the mountain fires. For, though the lava had not touched her to set her aflame, the volcanos' refuse lay around her feet, lava boulders scattered as far as one cared to look, spewed out by the Voda Cul in a tidal flood when the blocked river had finally broken free: black, twisted rock lying now all around the foot of Blackcob's stumpy hill. And the settlement itself covered with ash, the ruined houses and sheds, the rooftops gray as death, and the ash still drifting down like dirtied snow.

Skeelie and Berd were unsaddling, Berd's pale beard catching in the harness as he leaned forward. The two young soldiers were bringing hay. Skeelie stared with dismay at the patched fences and sheds, at the great patch of blackened boulders below, ruining the town's whitebarley fields and gardens. She paid no attention to Berd watching her, she could have been alone, felt far too upset by the condition of Blackcob and by her premonitions about Ram, to be civil to anyone.

No one knew where Ram was, she could not sense him now as she had so short a time ago, but the feeling that he would come was intense; and her awful sense of pain remained, pain soon to be known; and she felt she could not face its coming.

Maybe she was imagining it, maybe the fighting and strain of these last days had put wild ideas into her head, maybe Telien was not the same girl at all. But she knew better, knew Ram would come and that with his coming something in her life would change, would die; that she would be truly alone. And—it seemed to her that something terrible waited, something beyond her own pain, but she could not sense its shape, could not put a name to it.

Curse the fettering destruction of their Seers' powers. The sense of strength she had felt in the ruins, when Ram was freed at last of Burgdeeth, the power she had sensed then when they had all beheld that vision—now it seemed to be fading. What had it been, that power? *Was* it a strength of the mountain, fading now that those thundering peaks had quieted? A vision would come so suddenly, then be cut away again. Maybe . . . did it come clear while BroogArl's attention was focused elsewhere, perhaps? While he was strung taut with the conflict of some battle? Did Pelli raid Farr and Aybil, too? Perhaps for supplies? Was it only then, preoccupied, that BroogArl loosed his powers? And then, in his sudden rousing to their increased strength, did he lay hard on them again to destroy that strength?

And the sense of something else bothered her, too. As if someone else were blocking her powers of Seeing, someone . . . Was there something unfinished in Carriol? Was Jerthon hiding something from her, blocking her senses? But why would he? Oh, it was her imagination run loose. What would Jerthon hide from her, and why?

She removed her saddle with mechanical motions, plunging deeper into despair, turned away from Berd when he reached to take her saddle, his old, wrinkled face twisted with concern for her. She was rubbing saddle marks from her horse's back when a farmer standing high on his shed roof waved his hammer and shouted, "Winged one! Winged one and rider. A Seer . . ."

Skeelie stood frozen, saw one soldier running, saw Berd drop the saddles; she began to run too, toward the gray stallion winging down on the wind, dropping in silence between cottages. She saw Ram slide down, pale with fatigue. She felt the sense of Telien strongly. He was awash with concern for her. Telien, lying in a cave, hurt. She went to him then, began, with the soldier and Berd, to gather the stores he needed.

Mechanically, painfully, but with efficiency, she put into a pack herbs and salve, dried meat and new bread, roots, a pot to cook in, blankets, waterskins. She saw one soldier tying firewood into bundles, saw one preparing grain and feed. She worked dully, mechanically, caught in desolation.

When Ram stood looking down at her, prepared to depart, she could only look back at him and did not trust her voice to speak. His brown eyes were dark with pain—for Telien, but for her, too. And that made her feel worse. He pitied her, was trying to be gentle with her! She could not bear pity and gentleness, swallowed, could not speak. Choked back tears she would not let him see.

He extended his hand. "Friends, Skeelie? Skeelie . . . ?" He touched her arm. She turned away from him, then turned back with effort to look him straight in the eye.

"I hope she—that she will be well quickly, Ram. That you will care—care well for her." She took his hand then with a solemnity she had not intended and could not avoid. "Good-by, Ram. Ramad of wolves . . ."

She turned and walked away. She did not run until she was out of sight beyond the sheds. Then she ran straight down the hill to the river and among the boulders to a sheltered place, pushed her face against a boulder, choking back sobs until she could no longer choke them back, until she could not help the sobs that escaped her aching throat.

THE FLIGHT of the silver stallion was heavy now, loaded with bundles such as no winged one before him had ever had to suffer. Like a pack donkey, he let Ram know with some humor as he thundered aloft on straining wings. And Ram, so lost in remorse for Skeelie, so ridden with her pain, gave back little of humor, could only quip weakly that perhaps pack donkeys should grow wings.

The sun was low in the west, the dying afternoon stifling as heat rose from the cooling lava. Smoke drifted up, still, in the north between far peaks, and ash drifted down, burning Ram's throat and making Dalwyn cough. At last they winged over above the cave and dove for its lip—and on the lip of that drop, Telien stood poised as if she would step into empty space. Before her, nearly without foothold, Fawdref couched. Ram could feel the wolf's furious growl before he heard it.

The stallion remained motionless on the wind above her, weighted, struggling. One step and Telien would be over. Fawdref edged into her, forcing her back with bared teeth. She stared at him uncomprehending, and Ram felt her whisper, "They are waiting in the garden. I don't . . . *I must go to them!*" Ram tried wildly to reach her mind, to awaken her, and could not. Fawdref pushed her another step back. The stallion dropped down to the ledge, and Ram leaped clear, was beside her lifting her away, saw Rougier winging down from the sky then, answering Fawdref's summoning from some far distant grazing.

He laid Telien again on the stone shelf. Her ash-covered hair fell around her like dulled silver. She looked up at him blankly, her green eyes far away, seeing beyond him into—into what?

When he had stripped the packs from Dalwyn, seen the stallion leap skyward beside Rougier, he made a small fire, put a pot of water to boil, added herbs for tea, and began to prepare a meal for her. He laid out fresh bread and cold roasted meat, cicaba fruit that Skeelie had carried from Carriol, then put into his pack.

When the tea was ready, he led her to the fire. She knelt, held her hands to the warmth. Her eyes were softer now, very needing; she seemed so very frail. Yet beneath that frailty must lie an indomitable strength, to have brought her through that burning land; and, too, to have sustained her those long years living under AgWurt's rule. He poured out tea for her and held it so she could drink—strong, aromatic tea. "You were far away, Telien. Can you tell me where?

She pushed her hair away from her face, struggled to remember. "I was . . . it was spring, Ram. Suddenly it was spring, and I was in a garden in the center of a wood. But a dark, ugly garden, all in morliespongs and ragwort and beetleleaf, great dark leaves, and someone was calling to me, soldiers were watching me and I—I must . . ." she stopped, raised her eyes to him. "Where was I to go? What were they telling me to do?"

"Was there a building there in the garden?"

"A—yes! A dark hall, a terrible dark castle with *heads!* Its top was made of three huge heads! The eyes were windows, the mouths . . ."

He stared at her, chilled through. The Castle of Hape had touched her. BroogArl had touched her. But why?

Why? Because Telien would hold the runestone, was being drawn inexorably toward the runestone—being drawn into Time, the dark Seers pulling at her in their lust to have the stone.

Were *they* manipulating Telien into Time? Or were they simply following, like jackals, seeking to control her and so to take the stone?

He knelt beside her, tucked the blanket around her, and handed her the plate, found he was ravenous himself. Down in the cave the foal was playing while Meheegan ate of the grain Ram had brought, an expression on her face of wonderful pleasure and contentment. He watched Telien lay her meat on the bread in the Herebian way, taste it appreciatively, then fall to as if she had discovered quite suddenly how hungry she really was. But soon enough she seemed exhausted with the effort of eating, lay down with her head on his lap, her color gone. "What is it, Ram? What's the matter with me?"

Could it be the wound on her forehead? It was so like the one he had received as a child. That had made him dizzy and sick, though he was never certain how much of that misery was due to the wound and how much to the dark Seer's attacks on his mind. Attacks that had left him unconscious or delirious while his mind wandered in terrifying vastnesses.

"Ram, tell me what is happening to me."

"You have had a bad blow on the head. Did you fall?" He saw her nod imperceptibly. "But—but more than that, Telien. The ice and snow. You—you have stumbled out of Time. Into another time, somewhere . . . Just as I did once."

Meheegan looked up from eating. Telien watched the colt for a moment, in perfect harmony with the mother and foal. But her eyes were large with the fear that would not leave her. "I think, if you would tell me what happened to you that . . . maybe I would be less afraid."

He did not like telling her. And yet he had known he must, for she had a part in this. If it were still to happen to her, she had better know all she could. He moved close to her. She fit against him, warm, so close. She smelled of honey, he had never noticed that. Distracted, he brought his mind back with effort to his journey into Tala-charen, told her how he had gone there to find the runestone, meaning to stop the evil that Venniver wove in Burgdeeth, meaning to help free Jerthon and the slaves, meaning to battle the Pellian Seers in their increasing sweep of evil upon Ere. He told her how he and Skeelie and the wolves had climbed the icy mountains, fought the ice cat, the fire ogres, had come at last into the cave at the top of Tala-charen to face the dragon gantroed. How, when he found the runestone, it had split in white heat, and figures had appeared come out of time to take the shards. How he had seen Telien there.

She stared at him, swallowed, considered this. "I was there, Ram? I was in that place. But I have not been." She looked at him for a long time, as if she were memorizing his face. "Then—that is what is happening to me. I am falling through Time. The snow and ice, that was—I am being pulled back there—Tala-charen." She shuddered, took his hand. "I—I will see you there. Ramad the child . . ." She put her head against his shoulder, clung to him, trembling and cold. But when she lifted her face she seemed to have come to terms with it. "You—you cannot prevent it." It was not a question. "You . . ." She reached to stir the dying fire, then turned back to him smiling tremulously. "Tell me—tell me why you lived in Burgdeeth. You were a Seeing child. How did a Seeing child come there to Venniver, to that cruel man? Tell me about your life then, when you were small."

"I suppose I must start with the day I was born," he quipped.

"Yes," she said seriously. "Yes, that would be best, I think."

Evening was falling, the fire low. A faint breeze blew down to them from the mouth of the cave, and there was the dullest smear of moonlight behind the ashen sky. She settled into his arms once more and he began to tell her. "I was born a bastard. A bastard conceived of my mother's spite at being sold into unwanted marriage. I was deserted by my father before Tayba bore me. She found her way to a powerful old woman living alone on Scar Mountain. There in Gredillon's hut I was born and reared until I was eight." He drew the wolf bell from his tunic. The rearing bitch wolf shone softly in the muted moonlight. "Gredillon gave me this. It stood on her mantel. She put it into my hands minutes after I was born. She said I was born to it." At the sight of the bell Fawdref, dozing in shadow, spoke in muffled voice, a low, whining moan of pleasure. Telien touched the bell gently, tracing the line of the rearing wolf.

"As a small child, I called the foxes and jackals with the bell. When I was eight, the Seer HarThass, three days ride away in Pelli, discovered my skills and sent my father EnDwyl after me, to bring me to be trained as a Pellian Seer.

"Mamen and I ran away across the black desert toward Burgdeeth. EnDwyl followed us, riding out with an apprentice Seer on fast horses, overtook us as we were nearly into Burgdeeth. I—I called the wolves, then, Telien. In my fear of EnDwyl, I called the great wolves for the first time, called them down from the mountains to save us. It was . . ." He felt again that thrill, that overriding exaltation diminishing even his terrible fear of their pursuers. "The wolves came streaming down from the mountains, running like great shadows swiftly over the land. Fawdref was young then. Fierce as now. He . . . the wolves would have killed both men, had I not stopped them. EnDwyl held a knife at Tayba's throat. To save her, Fawdref set EnDwyl free."

He held her tight to him, aroused by the memory of fear, of that first time the wolves surged around him;

sharing this with her, aroused by Telien. He took her face in his hands. How perfect the bones. Her eyes were huge, so clear. Something in him had always been missing since that moment on Tala-charen. And now it was not missing.

She studied his face with great concentration. "When I was a child, Ram, before my mother died, I used to dream of someone—I was always alone, even with other children. I felt as if I were waiting for someone.

"When I grew older, when AgWurt brought our band up into Kubal, I . . . the men treated me badly. But always I thought there was someone who would not. Who would *care.* Who would know how I felt without my speaking of it, who would be . . ."

When he kissed her, they belonged to the mountain, belonged to Ere's moons, to the stars reeling and to Ere's winds: belonged to that vortex in Time when time mattered not.

HE WOKE BEFORE DAWN with a sense of intense pleasure, then was twisted awake and plunged into terrible dread by a clear vision. Carriol was at war, engaged in a battle unlike earlier attacks, a battle in which all in Carriol fought the dark Seers. He sat up, flinging the covers back, Saw the attack all across Carriol, every little farm and croft, Saw Jerthon's battalion riding hard—but away from Carriol! He stared into the darkness, Saw where Jerthon rode, *straight for Pelli!* Fast and heavily armed. Three battalions remained in Carriol and they battled the fierce Herebian attacks in skirmishes all across Carriol's fields and woods. Ram rose, felt the emptiness suddenly, turned back to the stone shelf, and saw that Telien was gone.

He lit tinder, stared around the cave, saw the wolves lined up at the cave mouth and felt their voices, felt Meheegan's voice. Yes, Telien was gone. Gone utterly. Gone not only from this place, gone out of Time itself, gone this instant as he woke—and they could not prevent it. Ram leaped for the cave mouth shouting her name, spun around to stare back into the cave in bewilderment, snatched up the wolf bell and sent his power winging out to find her—felt no breath of her. "Telien! *Telien!*" He drove with every strength he possessed to surge across space and time seeking Telien.

He could touch nothing but emptiness.

At last he subsided into cold defeat, and then the battle in Carriol engulfed him once more, against his will. Fawdref came to him, mourning Telien with opaque, distant-focused eyes; but alarmed, too, by the battle, tense with it as a wolf is tense stalking prey.

And now Ram began to sense that all across Ere Seers were stirring to the call of battle. He gripped the wolf bell, trying to force clarity to the breath of vision he touched, saw at last dark leaders raise their eyes as the harsh vibrations of battle touched their twisted minds; for this battle had to do with them, this balance of evil and light to do with them. Slowly Ram felt the slippery and the watchful reach out toward the dark wood, to bring their forces under the powers of Hape.

And he sensed that all across Ere gentle Seers, too, Seers who had moved unrecognized among men, hidden in fear, had begun at last to yearn again, to test their unused powers, to stand taller, to shake off their fear of discovery and listen with widening senses. And they, too, reached out toward Pelli—but, cowards too long, they were now afraid to bring their powers to battle the Pellian Seers, and they paused, ridden by confusion. They might have helped Jerthon, might have laid themselves unto a stronger master and thrown their forces with Jerthon; but they were too weakened by their own failures, too afraid.

Ram shouted for Dalwyn, laid his hand on Fawdref's head. Fawdref stared at him with an inexplicable look.

Ram knelt, threw his arms around the shaggy, beloved neck, stayed so in silence for a long moment, heard the commotion at the mouth of the cave then and rose to join Dalwyn—but a great band of winged ones was descending, and only slowly did he understand what was happening, only belatedly see a huge band of wolves streaming down the mountain: Fawdref's small family tribe and more; the entire band of the great wolves. They must have come from caves all over the mountain, perhaps had been waiting in the mountain for the fires to cool, must have gathered at their leader's call, for they glanced again and again at Fawdref as they moved down, their tongues lolling, their eyes keen and predatory. Ram stood stricken with wonder as they surged down the mountain and then, by ones and twos, by half a dozen at a time, began to jump to winged backs as the horses of Eresu swept in close to the ledge: wolves leaping to crouch between the horses' great wings. He saw Fawdref leap past him and settle between the wings of a dark mare, saw wolves riding in the sky in a spectacle that left him numbed. And he understood: it was their battle, too. The defeat of the Hape belonged to them, to all of them, not to men alone.

Dalwyn was there, snorting, eager, his eyes like fire. Ram swung onto his back, he leaped clear of the mountain; they were windborne, a surging mass of winged ones sweeping into the morning sky, wings spread across miles of sky. They swept over the scorched earth then across green hills as the morning light came brighter, across woods like dark seas below them. When they crossed the river Urobb where it flowed into Pelli, the winds were high and cold, buoying a hundred pair of wings. They swept above sheep fields and crofts toward the dark wood, and saw beyond it the cold sea.

Below them rose the dark castle surging with battle that raged across her fetid gardens and up the castle walls.

The scream of horses and the clash of swords came sharp on the wind, and new bands of Pellian soldiers were riding fast out from the dark wood. The Hape had taken the form of an immense lizard, twisted around the castle itself, its three heads snatching up men and tossing them like sticks: head of horned cat, head of toothed snake, head of eel tearing at the soldier's flesh. Dalwyn dropped suddenly upon the writhing lizard. Ram leaped, was clutching one scaly neck. Around him, winged horses dove and wolves jumped for the lunging coils, clinging, tearing at its scaly hide. Ram's knife flashed. The Hape reared, swelled in size, grew so huge the castle was nearly hidden beneath its writhing coils. Ram rode the scaly neck, trying to sever the cat-head, and the Hape's power was like hands tearing him away.

Below him, mounted soldiers slashed at the Hape, arrows flew, piercing its thick hide; swords were more useful than arrows as the soldiers rode in under its coils to slash at the softer belly. Ram felt Jerthon's strength suddenly from somewhere—he was not in this lizard battle, was somewhere dark, sending his power out to Ram. Ram felt the wolves' indomitable stubbornness as they fought; saw wings sweep above him and hooves slash as the winged ones themselves attacked the Hape, carrying two dozen Carriolinian troops. A winged horse screamed, swords flashed to cut at the Hape, dodging claws. Below, the battle was a melee; wolves were falling from the flailing snake down into the battle.

At last Ram clung alone as the winged ones surged around him dodging the Hape's lashing heads while soldiers slashed out. Blood spurted. Ram had almost severed the cat-head when the other two heads swung toward him and the toothed eel reached to clutch at him, the eel-head horrifying, grinning, mouth open to devour. Below, soldiers were climbing now, straddling the whipping lower coils; and Ram could sense soldiers below in the dark rooms, sense Jerthon there battling in darkness. He worked frantically at beheading the neck to which he clung, slipping in the spurting blood.

All but spent, Ram felt the last neck sinews sever, saw the cat-head fall, felt the Hape weaken as blood spurted anew from the neck. He could feel the dark Seers' forces gathered in surging hatred as the Hape writhed wildly, one neck headless and flailing, splattering blood, the eel-head coming down on him to tear him apart. He felt himself slipping and grabbed the severed neck bone, the only handhold, faced the eel-head in desperation and saw it had changed to a huge grinning head of a man.

Below in the castle Jerthon and two dozen troops routed Seers from locked rooms, tearing open bolted doors with a battering post; then turned suddenly to face torch-swinging Pellian troops. The battle was brutal in the half-dark, the torch fires swinging to show face of enemy, of friend, then swinging so only dark shadow lay before a man's sword. A grim, desperate battle waged in the close, fetid dark. Jerthon's men fought with a fierce hatred of that dark, fought with righteous fury until at last not a Pellian soldier remained standing, until all around their feet lay the dead and dying. Jerthon's men swept past them to fling open farther doors down darker hallways. "Take no captives! he shouted. "Kill them all, we want no captives such as these!" Not captives with Seer's minds to trick them, not in this desperate bid for victory. And as doors were flung open, monsters slithered out, abominations leaping to embrace them—monsters cut down by Jerthon's men, or sent trembling back to disappear when he held the runestone high before them.

And then in the cellars at last they came upon Broog-Arl secreted, as if he feared failure, among shadows; cringing. He stood suddenly, naked of flesh in a wild vision, white bone wielding a sword like flame, his sightless eye-holes seeing too clearly the stone in Jerthon's hand. Jerthon dropped the jade quickly into the pouch at his waist. And dangling from BroogArl's neck were the bloody heads of a dozen Carriolinian soldiers, comrades fallen in battle. BroogArl raised white bony hands and brought forces down upon Jerthon and Pol that drove them to their knees. They sought to rise, sweating, straining.

The two powers held equal for a long moment; Jerthon was hardly aware of the battle above, so desperately did he bring his powers against BroogArl. But BroogArl's force held Jerthon's sword frozen. Jerthon strained, sweating, until at last the bone-man gave way for an instant and Jerthon leaped on him, splitting his skull with one blow, severing the head so it lay at his feet like a halved apple, gleaming white. Then it darkened, turned once more to BroogArl's bearded head, split horribly, grinning in the last spasm of death.

And above the castle, as if the Hape and BroogArl were one, Ram at the same moment severed the snake-head. Both heads fell, BroogArl and snake, the dark powers mortally wounded and trying in desperation to rally, trying in desperation to change the Hape into another body; but failed to change it. And now all across Ere, as the dark Seers strove to buoy the Hape's powers, the timid Seers began at last to come together in sudden resolve, to reach out toward Pelli, to lend the Carriolinians their strength. And that added force maddened the Hape further so it surged with its own last strength in leaping fury and rose uncoiling into the sky, its two severed necks bleeding, its man-face laughing horribly. It tore away treetops in its frenzy, ran wildly in the sky, and it was winged: leathery wings beating the wind. Ram clung to its neck, his hands slipping in blood. The wind tore at him, the

Hape writhed, trying to unseat him. And then the winged ones came surging, darkening the sky, and from their backs riders shouted and swords flashed out.

The Hape flew lurching toward the sea. Ram gripped the slippery, bloody body, looked down at the rushing land, dug his knees deeper but was slipping, clung desperately to the severed neck. The wind nearly pulled him off, wind like giant hands tearing at him as the monster sped over Pelli's coastal city. And now Ram could sense Jerthon and Pol, a second wave of soldiers leaping into the sky above the castle to follow the Hape, could sense as a wild dark melee the battle that surged around the base of the castle itself where Carriolinians and Pellians fought to take possession of the castle now that all inside it were dead; he caught a vision of the wolves fighting alongside mounted soldiers, wolves leaping to pull dark riders from their mounts. And then the winged ones were crowding the Hape's flight closer so it clawed in the air and screamed.

They were over the sea, it rolled and churned below them. And Ram stared down at that wild water and knew, suddenly and coldly, that the Hape meant to dive into it, and he was filled with fear. For an instant everything seemed to pause, and then the Hape drove straight down toward the sea. Fury engulfed Ram. He cut hard into the thick hide until the Hape bellowed with pain and shivered the length of its body. But still it dove for the sea in a paroxysm of rage. Ram saw the sea coming fast, then was swallowed by it, tumbling in churning water, down, down, as the Hape twisted and thrashed. Ram kicked out, trying to free himself from the thrashing coils. The foaming surface above, dimly lit, seemed miles away. He could never hold his breath long enough to reach it, already his lungs were bursting. The Hape fought blindly, lashing the sea into storms. Ram tried to swim away from it, to fight upward, was suffocating. He had to breathe, had to. Shadows appeared above him, striking fear through him anew; then he saw that they were men. Suddenly he felt hands take him. He must breathe, must suck in air. Someone was lifting him through the churning water. The Hape's tail thrashed at them, nearly tore them apart. Jerthon—was it Jerthon there above him?

Yes, Jerthon. With terrible effort Jerthon pulled him free of the Hape; it roiled below them now so the water heaved and tore at them. Then the Hape grasped Jerthon in its claws and was pulling them down again. Jerthon pushed Ram free; someone dove past Ram. He *had* to breathe. He struck out feebly toward Jerthon, could see nothing clearly, knew he must suck water into his dying lungs; felt himself pulled upward again and began to kick in a feeble attempt to lift himself up.

He broke surface, sucked in air wildly, clutched at air, tried to call for Jerthon and could only gasp, knew he must dive for Jerthon. The sea was wild with the Hape's thrashing, red with blood. Hands were pulling at him. He could not see Jerthon. He lost consciousness.

He woke heaving, throwing up water as someone pummeled him, rough hands pushed water out of him. He twisted around and sat up, searching blindly.

Jerthon stood over him, soaking wet, his tunic ripped into shreds. Ram shouted with relief at seeing him, tried to rise and went dizzy.

Only slowly did Ram sense Jerthon's chagrin, understand the pain of his expression. Something was wrong. Very wrong. He could not read the sense of it, stared at Jerthon's shredded tunic, was wildly glad Jerthon was alive, stared at the torn leather pouch where the runestone of Eresu had lain.

The bottom of the leather pouch was ripped away. The leather hung limp and empty.

Jerthon's look was dark, full of misery. He could not speak for some time. Ram dared not speak, dared not ask. When Jerthon did speak at last, his voice was tight and stilted. "It is—the runestone is in the sea."

Ram rose, stood dripping and cold, dizzy. The runestone could not be lost. Not in the sea. Not . . .

"It is lost," Jerthon said, his eyes miserable.

"I thought—I thought you would drown. How did you get out? You saved my neck down there."

"Drudd pulled me out, pulled us both out," Jerthon said, dismissing it.

Ram turned to stare at the sea. Its breakers plunged and rolled steadily. Only a pink-tinged swirl could be seen where the Hape had been. Only very slowly could he bear to face the loss of the stone. "The runestone: in . . . In the sea? But the—the Hape will have it then, it . . ."

"The Hape is weak, Ram, nearly dead. If we—if we can defeat BroogArl's forces completely, I think the Hape—with no strength from BroogArl's men to draw into itself, I think the Hape may die."

Ram stared at him, trying to collect his senses. To defeat Pelli, to prevent the Hape taking the stone . . . He stood at last, rallying himself. "Let's get on with it. We've a war to win." He gave the signal to mount. "I will ride behind you if Dalwyn can carry us both."

Girded with fury at the loss of the stone, the band came down on the castle in wild force, joined with the troops there. They cornered Pellians against the castle wall and slaughtered them. They drove hard into the wood and found troops hiding, wounded, tired of battle, and slaughtered them. No Pellian could be let to live and use, if he carried Seer's blood, his dark powers against them.

And the wolves killed many, fighting by the soldier's sides, leaping, tearing, enjoying the attack in all their animal lust. When the battle had done, when not a Pellian could be found alive, the great band of wolves came all around Ram and stood looking up at him with bloody muzzles, grinning.

It was then Ram saw the tall white-haired figure slipping away into the wood. He swung around, staring. "*That* one, Fawdref! Where did he come from?"

The dogwolf looked at him a moment, licking blood from his lips before he answered. *He came out of the wood and fought beside us, Ramad. He is fierce as a wolf himself. He came out of a time you are yet to touch, moves driven by the winds of Time in a way he can seldom control. He is a lonely man. Lonely.*

Ram stared at the wolf's knowing eyes and felt his spirit lift suddenly with hope. Hope for Telien; for if Anchorstar moved on the winds of Time, then Anchorstar moved in the realms where she had been swept, and perhaps he could touch her there. "I will speak with him, I will summon him!" Ram cried, wild with his sudden need.

The great wolf moved close to Ram, pressing his shoulder against him, laid his head against Ram's arm. *He is gone, Ramad.*

And though Ram searched the wood, there was no sign of Anchorstar or the dun stallion. Gone. Gone into Time. Why had Anchorstar come here, why had he fought here?

Jerthon's troops stormed the castle, searching for stragglers they might have missed, holding back in secret rooms; and he and Ram came at last to the cellars. Jerthon turned BroogArl's body over with his toe, thought of burying it, shook his head. "BroogArl can end in flame like his castle. Let's get out of here, the smell of him makes me choke."

"Jerthon, *did* we kill them all?"

Jerthon gave him a long look, touched unthinking the place in his tunic where the runestone had ridden, glanced down, his face dark with its loss. "Kill them all, Ram? What do you feel?"

They stood silently then, sensing out into Pelli, into all of Ere for that feel of dark that had ridden so long with them. After some moments their faces began slowly to lighten; they looked into each other's eyes with hope flickering, then with a rising sense of victory. There was no trace of the evil now, no sense of BroogArl's retinue, or of the cloying dark that had been the Hape. A sense of scattered, dark Seers, yes, drawn together at this time in their hatred of the light; but Seers separated by their own selfish ways, their own despotic little hierarchies, and as opposed to one another as quarreling snakes. There was no sense, with BroogArl and the Hape gone, of unity among those who were left.

"Kill them all, Ram?" Jerthon's fatigue had left him. He lifted his head in triumph. "I hope perhaps we have. Killed all the power that resided *here*."

Ram's hope had lifted to wing outward as he examined the cool absence of massed evil. He wanted to shout suddenly, he embraced Jerthon with wild joy. "And the runestone—we will dive for it!"

Jerthon looked chagrined. "Dive, Ram? The sea in this place is deeper than any man can think to go. *We* were deeper than I would have thought possible. The stone . . . but perhaps we will think of a way."

Ram gripped Jerthon's shoulder. "The stone is gone, but *we* are not! We have won, man! We've destroyed the Pellian monsters!" And yet, as he tried to cheer Jerthon at the loss of the stone, beneath his own bravado lay a heaviness that would not subside. For the loss of the stone, yes. But the real pain there, like a dull knife wound, was for the loss of Telien.

Jerthon, seeing his pain, cuffed him and grinned. "Come, then, Ramad of wolves. Let's make an end to this den of Hape. Come, watch the roasting while we bury the monsters in flame!"

They went up the dark stairways and into the dim hall, where Jerthon's men were throwing the furniture into a great heap, stacking on logs from the castle's firewood, building a tall pyre. In the upper rooms, the shutters were flung open to act as a chimney.

Jerthon took up a torch from those stacked beside the castle door, struck flint, and when the torch flared he lighted the pyre. Timbers and furnishings caught at once and began to burn hot and quick, the flame leaping upward in the draft from the windows above, the main hall soon so hot it drove them out through the wide double doors.

They stood in the murky wood watching as the Castle of Hape was consumed in flame. The winged ones crowded close to the soldiers, not liking fire, glancing again and again toward the sky as the flames leaped higher.

At last the castle's stone walls began to crumble. The wolves pushed closer together, and Fawdref came to Ram. Ram stood abstracted, his hand on the dog wolf's head, watching the burning of the castle until the old wolf began to nudge and push at him. No sensible wolf lingered near a fire in forest land. And no sensible man, either, Fawdref let him know. Ram knelt before the great wolf, but Fawdref drew back his lips at the rising flame and nudged Ram until he rose and backed away from the fire. And then, as if they could bear the fire no longer, the winged ones stirred and leaped suddenly skyward like hawking birds and were away toward the dark mountains.

The wolves pushed together in a great band to crowd around Ram, eager, too, to be away. Ram pulled Fawdref to him, reached to touch Rhymannie, was loathe to let them go, imagined with a sense of loss the great wolves streaking silently away up through Ere's forests toward the Ring of Fire.

Chapter Nine

And suddenly, clearly, Ram knew that he must go with them. Must return to the cave where Telien had been. Must seek her first in that place. And were there secret runes in the old caves there that would tell him how to span Time? How to take himself into the spinning center of Time where Telien had gone?

Chapter Ten

TELIEN, swept like a chip in Time's leaping river, could not stop herself. Her mind reeled with a hundred places tumbling one atop another, with cities, with voices and faces and smells jumbled. And then suddenly she sensed that someone was with her, reaching out to her. A girl, someone close, someone caring—someone who seemed like a sister. She had never had a sister. She felt tears come in her eyes at the sudden touch of warmth, this sense of someone young and caring reaching out to push away the terrifying loneliness, to push back the vast reaches of Time. For Skeelie had reached out to her, and Telien clung to that sense of strength with terrible desperation.

Skeelie had been resting after battle, exhausted, dirty, starved, when she began to think strongly of Telien.

All across Ere troops had battled the forces of the dark Seers, forces boiling out of the hills, small dark bands riding fast out of isolated camps to wield destruction across Carriol, just as Jerthon laced destruction down upon the Castle of Hape. That had been Jerthon's secret. She had Seen at last, and known. And Ram had known. She and Berd and Erould and the men of Blackcob had joined Carriol forces in mid-battle up the Somat Cul, pursuing stolen horses, cutting down dark raiders. And, as in Pelli Broog-Arl had died, and then as the Hape's body had died, the forces that Skeelie's band battled had diminished. Without the dark powers to force them back, Carriol's troops had begun to slaughter the Herebian in a wholly satisfying manner, had driven them out until not a raider remained on Carriol soil alive. And the dark blocking had pulled back, and Skeelie had Seen, not only the battle in Pelli but the battles that flared up across other parts of Carriol, battles being won now by Carriol's troops.

Yes, she thought bitterly, Jerthon had shielded his knowledge of that attack on Pelli from her. He had kept it secret—in order to shield the knowledge from Ram. In order to give Ram his moments with Telien, undisturbed. She bit her lip with fury, with pity for Telien, with emotions she could not sort out. Had Jerthon known that Telien's time was so short?

Skeelie and old Berd, his white beard flying, and Erould with blood running down his dark hair, had fought shoulder to shoulder the dark Herebians high in the loess hills until those still able to ride had fled from them.

Now the men, sensing no new attack, sensing with growing eagerness the feel of victory in Pelli, had gone downriver to rest and to care for their mounts. Skeelie, alone in an isolated bend of the river, stripped to the buff and washed away the white loess dust, the sweat and blood of battle, had rinsed out her clothes and sat now shivering as they dried over a hastily built fire. Her cuts burned. One sword wound along her arm was deeper. She laced it with birdmoss from the riverbank, to soak away the poison. She bet she was a pretty sight, all scarred. But who was to see? Who would care? She could hear the men's voices downstream, and the voices of the women farther upstream.

And, sitting before the fire, her thoughts were pulled away from her suddenly. She Saw Telien in a clear vision, knew Telien intimately. Was angered at first by Telien's presence in her mind, wanted only to be rid of her. But Telien's fear became her fear, she knew the girl's terror as if it were her own, knew in every detail Telien's confused journey into the malestrom of Time, was stricken suddenly with a terrible empathy for Telien and reached out to her at last, knew she must go to her.

She tried, forced her powers out away from her own time into Time itself. But as suddenly as it had come, the vision vanished from her, and she could not sense Telien at all. She tried desperately, again and again, and failed. Failed Telien, and so failed Ram.

She turned away at last, wanting to weep and unable to weep, weary and very much alone.

When the sense of someone there with her, supporting her, vanished, Telien was more alone than ever, cut adrift again in the eternal vastness of Time, unable to know, any more, what future or past was: she was swept on an endless sea in which she could find no bearing, find nothing to cling to, nothing to tell her, even, who she was.

Who had touched her mind so briefly? So welcome. A girl, but who? As close as a sister, someone . . . the loss of that brief encounter sickened her further, set her adrift again utterly, more chaotically than before.

She stood in a rough field. She remembered a rushing city moments before where she had wandered the streets among crowds, seen men strung from crosspoles and cut open like oxen, butchered for pleasure because they were Seers. Terror accompanied her. She knelt in the little field, trembling, her very will all but gone.

Her mind reeled with a hundred generations, a hundred sights. She had seen women and children kept like animals while ruling Seers wallowed in luxury, seen fields and towns burned with the fires of the mountains flooding down and the people kneeling amidst the burned land to supplicate the gods. Seen men enslaved and driven mad at the pleasure of corrupt rulers.

She raised her face to stare at the field and was suddenly not in the field, but in near-darkness—in a small, dark space, damp and close, and strong with the sense of death. She touched a wall, shivered. As she grew accustomed to the near-dark, she could make out a man lying at the far side of the cave. She knew that he was dying.

He spoke, startling her anew, spoke in a rasping whisper. She did not want to hear that voice, did not want to listen; but knew she must listen, was horrified, was compelled by some force to listen, felt she almost knew what he would say. The smell of dying mingled with the damp smell of the cave. His voice was faint. His words made her shiver. "*A bastard child will be born . . .*" She trembled, covered her ears, could not block out his voice.

"*A bastard child will be born. And he will rule the wolves as no Seer before him has done . . .*" He was speaking of Ram, surely. How could it be that he could speak of Ram? In what time was she? In what place? "*A bastard child fathered by a Pellian bearing the last blood of the wolf cult. My blood! My blood seeping down generations hence from some bastard I sired and do not even know exists!*

"*A child born of a girl with the blood of Seers in her veins. A child that will go among the wolves of the high mountains, where the lakes are made of fire. Wolves that are more than wolves. And that boy will seek a power greater even than the wolf bell, a power that even I could not master.*"

Telien drew in her breath. The runestone! Surely he spoke of the runestone!

The man had stopped speaking. He coughed, lay with his life draining away. She went to him, repelled by him, yet drawn to him beyond her will. She touched him once, shivered uncontrollably, leaped up and ran from the cave—and was running fast through a sunlit wood, running in terror from that wasting corpse that lay, now, somewhere in distant time.

She stopped herself with effort. It did no good to run. She crouched down into a fetal position in a patch of sun between trees. She had nothing to hold to. Nothing. She wanted Ram, wanted him to tell her what was happening to her. She wanted him to hold her so she could not be swept away, never again be swept away.

The wood vanished. She was in another cave. But this was a high domed cave, and light. A hairy gantroed like a great bristling dragon lay wounded across the floor; and the earth was rocking; thunder filled her ears.

A dark-haired young boy stood beside the gantroed. She did not understand who he was, but his very presence made her heart pound. Then she saw the round stone in his cupped hands, a stone glowing deep green, and she understood. *Ram! Ramad!* She stared at him with terrible need, with terrible longing for this child who was Ram.

The fire struck suddenly, a long jagged bolt of brilliant light. The jade orb turned white hot. It shattered, lay in nine long shards in Ram's cupped hands. And the mountain trembled again, and a long jagged scar opened in the floor of the cave and the dragon gantroed began to slip down into it. Then, as the jade in Ram's hands began to cool and deepen in color, Telien saw other figures appear out of nowhere around Ram. And Ram looked up at her once, puzzled, as if he should know her; and in her hands lay one slim green shard of the shattered runestone of Eresu.

The cave faded. She clutched the stone, trembling, crying out to Ram though he could not hear her. She gripped the stone to herself and knew that she must give it to Ram. That she must, through all of Time, return to Ram with the runestone.

She stood on a mountain meadow in sunlight and suddenly she saw Ram again. But he was a very little boy now, red-haired, running in the wind carrying the wolf bell, laughing, followed wildly all around by foxes running. *Ram! Ramad!* She could not reach or speak to him, and he faded. Then she saw him once more, a little older, his hair dyed black. Saw him running again, but now in fear across a vast black desert, leading a trotting pony, followed by a dark-haired, beautiful woman. She saw men riding hard after them. She saw Ram and the woman turn, in a wood, to face their pursuers. *Ram would be killed!* She heard him call the wolves then, in a strange rhyming voice, and saw the wolves come streaming down the mountain to leap and kill . . .

And she heard Ram's voice suddenly, deep, as she knew it. Close to her. Imperative. "*Telien! Telien!*"

She stared around frantically, reaching out, but he was not there. Her own voice died on Time's winds as she cried out for him, and she was swept away again into darkness.

She was so tired. Despondent. So close to Ram, his voice so close, and then to be swept away. She clutched the jade to her, sick with fatigue. So confused. She must rest or she would die, must drink. She leaned against the dirt wall of—Was she back in the cave with the dying Seer? Where was she?

Did it matter where she was, or in what time she stood? She was so thirsty, wanted water, wanted to lie down. As she turned, her hand brushed a hollow in the wall. She raised her face to it blindly. Could there be water seeping out? She reached in cautiously. But it was only a dry little niche. Suddenly, too sick to hold the jade any longer, trembling, she laid it there in the niche, far back, then huddled down on the floor against the earthen wall, shivering, wanting only to sleep, to be left alone.

"*Telien! Telien!*"

She did not hear his voice. She slept, gone in exhaustion.

"Telien!" But he could not reach her.

When she woke at last, she was curled up just as she had been in the close dark, but now lay on an open expanse of stone with the wind icy, the evening sky darkening so stars had begun to burn cold in its icy blue. She was freezing cold, stood up, huddling against the rising hill behind her, to stare around her. Far away she could see jagged mountains. She was on a bare plateau. Space fell to her left, and on the rocky hill behind her stood five huge trees, ancient and twisted.

"Telien!" She spun around, nearly fell. His voice was only a whisper, but real! She stared around expecting to see him, saw nothing but stone and emptiness. His voice was in her mind, only in her mind. She stood barely breathing, tears flooding down.

Ram had ridden hard to keep up with the fleeing wolves, for they seemed bent on reaching the mountains in one day's run. The Pellian mount he had taken was nearly spent. He stopped at last beside a clump of small trees to rest the poor beast. Fawdref and Rhymannie alone remained with him, urging the rest of the pack away, for their very presence in the lowlands seemed a discomfort to them. As evening fell, he tended the horse, built a supper fire, then stood at the edge of the cliff staring out into the vast northern reaches, at the jagged peaks of the Ring of Fire standing black in the falling light. And suddenly he felt her there beside him. "Telien! Telien!" And yet the ledge was empty. Distraught, frantic, he shouted to her, oblivious to all else but the sense of Telien come so suddenly to him.

He shouted over and over into the falling night, but now she was gone again, he could sense nothing of her now, there was only emptiness. The thin moons hung dull in the ash-clouded sky, lonely and bleak.

From Time indecipherable he had sensed her there, standing in the same place he stood, Telien there beside him on the ledge, her presence so close. And then she was gone.

When he turned away at last in anguish, in rising fury at powers he could not control, he saw Anchorstar. Anchorstar, standing motionless beside the fire between Fawdref and Rhymannie, his white hair catching the firelight. Anchorstar come out of Time in this empty place, standing still as stone, his eyes seeking Ram's, his face stern and drawn.

AND IN THE NORTH of Carriol, Skeelie remained alone by the river as the soldiers made camp. She tried again with an effort that left her exhausted to move into Time, to touch Telien. She went dizzy and sick with the effort, reached, felt Time like a river swirling away from her so no matter how she reached, came close to it, thought she had thrown herself into its current, it slipped aside and was gone; she could not touch Telien. She gave it up at last, defeated.

RAM WENT TOWARD ANCHORSTAR, stood facing him across the fire. The wolves had turned, moved around the fire toward Ram, but they watched Anchorstar without enmity, comfortable with him. Where had Anchorstar come from? Out of nowhere in this desolate place: out of Time unimaginable. Where had he traveled since he had battled beside Fawdref at the Castle of Hape, a few hours ago? How many years had he traveled? Had he come to speak to Ram of Telien? Did he know . . . ? Ram's voice was hoarse with eagerness. "You have something to say, you . . ."

Anchorstar stopped him with lifted hand. His drawn face was cold. "Yes. She is there in Time, Ramad, yes. I know that she is there. But I have not seen her, nor touched her path through Time. She . . . Time is infinite, how could I expect . . ."

"But the starfires! You . . ."

"The starfires, yes. I have never been sure whether they are a help to me in trying to—to return to my own time, or whether—whether it is they that speed my headlong fall. I am loathe to cast them away. They were given me by someone trusted. He said they would help to guide me home. Telien—she carries one now, Ramad, in the pocket of her tunic."

"Yes, you . . ."

"One I gave her because—I felt her need. Though perhaps . . . I knew, Ramad, that she would be sucked into Time. I thought that the starfire might bring her home again. And yet . . ."

"You are saying nothing! What power have those stones? How can I use them to follow her? You can show me! You . . ."

"I can do nothing. I am drawn and twisted through Time just as is Telien. I wish—I wish it were not so. I have tried. I have tried, and failed."

Ram's need rose to fury. "You cannot? Or you will not?" He drew around the fire to Anchorstar, stood facing him.

"You move in Time, Anchorstar! You will show me, or . . ." He had Anchorstar by the throat suddenly, forcing him back against boulders, his fist raised in a madness of desperation. "Show me, man! *You* can manipulate Time, move through Time!" Anchorstar did not resist him. The tall thin man did not struggle, but watched Ram with ever saddening expression. And even in his fury, Ram was ashamed to speak so to this man.

Anchorstar looked at him steadily. "You are as hot-headed a young warrior as they say you are. In my time they say . . ."

Ram drew back his fist. "You are wasting precious minutes!"

Anchorstar flared suddenly and swung, twisted Ram, held him in a grip like iron. "Back off your anger, Seer! And listen to me!"

Ram went limp in his hands, shocked at the man's power, waiting for a moment to take him off-guard. But Anchorstar loosed him, and Ram stepped back and did not fight Anchorstar. The tall man looked at him squarely. "When you called out to her, did you not think—did you not sense her here? *I* think she was here on this cliff. I think when you called out that she was here with us, but in a different time, Ramad. You would only have to move in Time to . . ." He searched Ram's eyes. "I cannot tell you *how.* You must use your own powers for that, Seer. I cannot tell in what time she stands here, but I feel that she is here. I sense her here as surely as *I* stand on this ledge.

"The starfires, then! They . . ."

Anchorstar drew the pouch from his tunic, opened it, and spilled three stones into Ram's open hand. Ram clenched his fist around them, wanting, needing Telien; and the wolves moved suddenly, raised their heads, and Fawdref's voice broke shrill on the night—and Anchorstar was gone. The wolves were gone. The night was empty. No fire burned, the sky was vaster, the light of the full moons falling clear and unbroken by ash.

The few small trees were gone. In their place rose five huge trees, centuries old.

The loneliness was overwhelming. He whispered her name into emptiness, "Telien. Telien," and prayed she would come to him and did not understand how he could expect that out of all time she could come to him; and then suddenly she was there clinging to him in desperation, pushing her face into the hollow of his neck, warm, so warm, her skin soft against him and smelling of honey.

He held her, sought every detail of her face, knew her mind and her fear and knew the terrible journey she had suffered, touched her and was unable to believe her presence, was terrified she would be gone again as Anchorstar had gone. "It was so long," she whispered. "So—so empty, Ram. You can't—you can't think what it's like. I . . . Hold me tighter. Hold me so I can't go back. Don't let me go, I can't go back if you hold me, it can't take me from you . . ."

But she was fading in his arms.

"*Telien!*"

He could not feel her in his arms, there was only emptiness, she was a cloud. She gripped him once with trembling fingers, was twisted away and fading, and was gone from his reaching arms.

The plateau was empty.

And when he turned away at long last, turned back to where a fire had once blazed, the full moons had taken a different position in the clear sky, and the great, ancient trees that had stood on the cliff were gone. Only a few saplings could be seen beginning to push above the tall, still grass.

JERTHON'S BATTALION RODE into Carriol in silence at dusk of the following day. The Hape was defeated. BroogArl was defeated, his Seers dead, the castle burned. The streets of Carriol were crowded, should have been wild with victory. There should have been shouting, singing. But all was silence. Carriol's men and women lined the streets in quiet attention as the battalion rode in. For in spite of victory, Ramad was gone from them.

The vision of his disappearance had come clear to

Tayba and to Skeelie, to the Seers who had stayed behind. Ram might return as abruptly as he had disappeared, but somehow the sense of his going seemed, to those Seers who had viewed it, one of terrible finality.

Jerthon knew that Tayba was not among the crowd, that she stood alone in the tower, in the solitide of her room—reaching out in vain toward Ram, across time she could not manipulate. Reaching out, and sorrowing, unable to touch him.

Had Ram been sucked into Time by powers yet unimagined? Or had he only, mourning for Telien, thrown himself into that maelstrom in search of her? Even with the vision of his going that had come so clear to them, the sense of Ram's feelings was not clear. All had happened too fast: an instant when Ram faced Anchorstar, an instant when it seemed he clung to Telien somewhere, and then he was gone.

Jerthon dismounted, left his horse to another to care for, and went up into the tower. Tayba would need him. She would be drawn tight inside herself and short with him in her grief over Ram; but she would need him now. He could not think what to say to her. But that did not matter.

Gone. Ram gone. He shook his head, trying to drive out the nightmare, but it would not go. Gone into Time. Had Ram found Telien in some realm so remote from this time that one could hardly imagine it? And did Telien have a shard of the stone, could the two of them, perhaps, with the power of the stone, yet return to their own time?

Or would they, foolish, young—valiant—try to seek out the rest of the stones across a warping vastness of Time that no man could truly comprehend? He came up the third flight and stood before Tayba's door, knew she was pacing. He knocked, heard her answer with muffled annoyance.

He found Tayba pacing, and Skeelie there, worn from

battle, from her swift journey home, kneeling before an old chest rummaging, muttering, her shoulders hunched beneath stained fighting leathers, her face, when she turned to look at him, pale with loess dust from the ride out of the north, her eyes haunted with the knowledge of Ram's loss. She said nothing, would not meet his eyes, was strung tight with the agony of her loss—loss to Time as well as to Telien. At last she pulled out a cloak of heavy wool from the chest, closed the lid, and sat back on her heels, lowering her eyes before him, then looking up at him suddenly and defiantly. "I am going there. I am going into the mountains, and please don't argue. To the caves of Owdneet first, to find runes I think can . . . can lead me. Can take me into Time, can . . . I will not rest until I have done this." And, seeing his scowl, "*Please* don't argue, Jerthon."

He looked at the two of them. Had Tayba encouraged Skeelie in this? No, he thought not. Skeelie's need was plain. Despite Ram's love for Telien, she would save him.

"What makes you think that in the caves—that you can find anything to help you?"

"I . . . when Ram and I were in the great grotto, when we were children, we . . . Fawdref showed us with his thoughts that there were caves there that held the old tablets and runes of the ancient city. There were powers written there, Jerthon. Powers lost to us."

"But powers of the gods, Skeelie. You can't . . ." He knew he argued uselessly. He would keep her here if he could, and knew she would not stay.

"Powers any Seer can use, Jerthon. If one is willing to seek them, willing to try them, to risk . . ."

"Yes. To risk death. Or worse than death."

She stared at him, defying him, her thin face drawn, her dark eyes large with anguish, as she had looked so often as a child. "You know I must go, and arguing only makes it harder." She rose to stand before him, hugged him suddenly in a terrible embrace, clung to him for a long moment. Hugged Tayba with more tenderness, then fled, turning at the door only to say, "I will come to you when I am ready to leave. Meanwhile—take care of her, Jerthon. Care gently for one another."

SKEELIE RODE OUT for the mountains early the next dawn, accompanied by the older Seer Erould. He would bring her horse back. Would, before he returned home, ride into Kubal as a trader. That had been Jerthon's idea, to know what was happening in Kubal. "To be sure *they* are not strengthening again. Erould, you crusty old dog," Jerthon had said, grinning, "you look the part of a trader. Tossle your hair, don't bathe. You'll do very well as a trader."

Skeelie and Erould rode in silence through the gray dawn up along the sea then along the river Somat Cul. Skeelie looked up toward the mountains rising ahead of them and saw, in her mind, the shadows of wolves, then the shape of the grottos of Owdneet. She pushed her horse faster, impatient to get on. And grown impatient, suddenly, of company, too, of conversation. Though she should be thankful for Erould's presence, for this last warm link with men familiar, men of her own time and her own kind. But she could not make conversation in spite of needing human warmth, she mourned Ram too much.

If Telien were dead—but she put that thought from her. She would save Telien, she loved Telien in a strange, puzzling way. Because of Ram, she supposed, though it made no sense to her. Jealous, pained at Telien's existence, yet she would care tenderly for her, would bring them both home, and gladly, if ever she could search them out.

Erould, his mind politely closed to her misery, pulled his cap down over his dark grizzled hair, then waved an arm to encompass the pale loess hills to the north. "Won't be long, all this will be settled. Farms, a little town. Now the Pellian's Seers are dead, the Hape. Oh, we will build, Skeelie. Grow crops—men will come from all over Ere, craftsmen, breeders of fine stock . . . ."

She didn't want to answer. Just let him keep talking. The sound of his voice was good, tying her to this time for a little while yet, tying her to warmth and human feeling—pushing away her fear of the unknown that she would soon face. Making her know that no matter where she was, in what dark reaches of Time, yet here in this time Carriol would be safe, would be filled with the joy of its growth.

And Ram might never see it. Would miss it all, the joyful work and growth. Ram. Ram. You loved it so—this time, this lovely land.

Erould watched her, touched her mind, then, in spite of himself and drew back pained with her pain, driven for a moment as she was driven, desperate in her mourning and need; so painful were her thoughts that he wished—not for the first time—that he had not the skill to touch another's mind. He knew where she was headed and why, mourned for her, was distressed for her, and could do nothing. He would not see her again in this life, he felt suddenly certain. He took pains to hide that thought from her. They came to Blackcob at noon, made a brief greeting, a brief meal, and went on. Skeelie had begun to grow nervy, her fear taking hold, thoughts of turning back beginning to rise unbidden. They rode in silence up along the Urobb, and that night camped in the lee of the dark mountains, the next day followed a goat trail so narrow and with so steep a drop beside it, it made them both nervous. Erould left her at last in midafternoon at the foot of the peak where lay the grotto of Owdneet, swung away leading her horse down in the direction of Kubal, left his good will with her and his prayers and did not look back.

Skeelie watched him go and swallowed. She stared down over the land, the lovely land. The hills above Burgdeeth and Kubal were blackened, scarred; but they would be green again. Even in a few weeks, she knew, the green would begin to come. In the far distance a gray smear showed the outline of Carriol's cliffs and the ruins; and the sea was a bright streak in the dropping sun. Lovely. She bit her lip. Would she see all this again?

Oh, maudlin girl! Do get on! What are you dawdling for? Maybe you can't even *find* a way into—a way . . . She set her jaw against fear, shouldered her pack, and began to climb up the old trail toward the grotto. Did the wolves know she was here, did they sense her? She could get no feel of them.

At sunset she stood ready to enter the mountain. She looked back over the land once more, softened in the falling light, took flint from her pack, and a lantern. She struck feeble light that lurched across the rock, adjusted the lantern, and entered the tunnel.

She journeyed through the dark tunnels, through caves, with only her lantern to lead her, came at last deep inside the mountain to the ancient grotto. It rose all in darkness touched only faintly by the last light of evening through its openings on the far wall; high openings, there near the distant ceiling. Here, twelve years before, she and Ram had stood. She knelt, stricken suddenly with the pain of remembering. She wept alone in the great grotto, wept for Ram.

At last she lifted her face, stared absently at the light-struck stone where her lamp stood. Had she come all this way only to weep? She rose and went on through the grotto and out another portal and up across a grassy hill. The moons had not yet risen. Her lantern guided her, catching at the tall, still grass. She stood at last, lantern raised to look, before the dark face of a building, made against the mountain, all of black obsidian. She entered into the great hall that was the second grotto. Here lay the hidden picture stones, the hidden parchments secreted by the gods in ages far past—in ages where she might yet stand this night, she thought, shuddering.

She began to search among the caves and small rooms, her lantern throwing arcs of light across the carven stone, searching for hidden doors, for passages. She felt into niches, into cracks in the natural stone, searching. She would find it, a parchment, a stone tablet, something bearing the runes of magic, something to unlock the secrets of Time. Something to help her bring Ram home. Ram—and Telien. She meant, fiercely, to find it. She would not leave these caves until she had; would leave them only in a time so far from this time—where Ramad was, where Ramad had been swept.